Against the Tide

CHOSEN DAUGHTERS

Wings like a Dove

by Christine Farenhorst

Dr. Oma

by Ethel Herr

Against the Tide

by Hope Irvin Marston

Against the Tide

The Valor of Margaret Wilson

Hope Irvin Marston

P U B L I S H I N G
P.O. BOX 817 • PHILLIPSBURG • NEW JERSEY 08865-0817

Scripture quotations are from The Holy Bible, King James Version, 1611.

Printed in the United States of America

Library of Congress Cataloging-in-Publication Data

Marston, Hope Irvin.
  Against the tide : the valor of Margaret Wilson / Hope Irvin Marston.
    p. cm. — (Chosen daughters)
  Summary: Late in the seventeenth century in Galloway, Scotland, where it is illegal to believe that Jesus Christ, not the king, is head of the church, Margaret Wilson, a stalwart young Covenanter, refuses to recant after being arrested by the king's forces, although her life is at stake.
  Includes bibliographical references.
  ISBN-13: 978-1-59638-061-5 (pbk.)
  1. Wilson, Margaret, 1667-1685—Juvenile fiction. [1. Wilson, Margaret, 1667-1685—Fiction. 2. Covenanters—Fiction. 3. Christian life—Fiction. 4. Presbyterian Church—Fiction. 5. Reformation—Fiction. 6. Scotland—History—1660-1688—Fiction.] I. Title.
  PZ7.M3567552Aga 2007
  [Fic]—dc22

                                                                    2007014793

Dedicated to
Sheena and Phil
&
Donna and Forrest

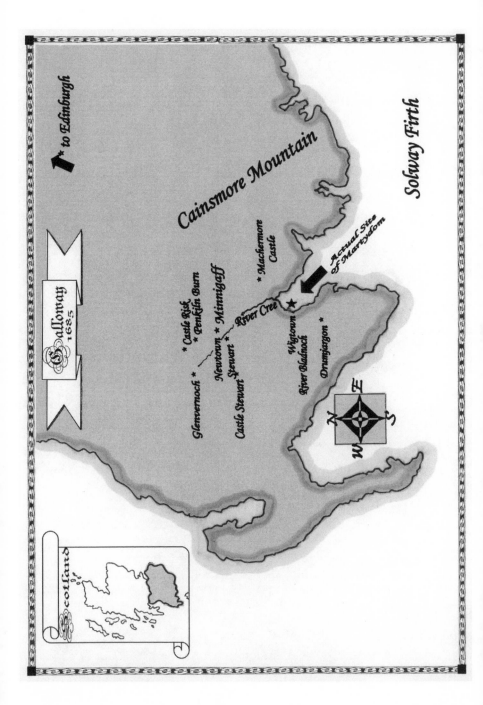

CONTENTS

ACKNOWLEDGMENTS

My interest in Scotland began with a pen pal named Sheena who lived in Dalry, Scotland. For at least sixty years, Sheena and I have shared our lives through letters. I first visited her and her husband, Phil Leadbetter, in Perth six years ago. Through the efforts of the Leadbetters, I met two people who graciously shared their vast knowledge of the Covenanters' struggles. In the spring of 2005, I interviewed the Rev. A. Sinclair Horne, secretary for the Scottish Reformation Society, in Magdalen Chapel, Edinburgh, a hallowed spot in Covenanting history.

Sheena and Phil directed me to a second authority in Wigtown, Donna Brewster. I spent four delightful days as a houseguest with Donna and her husband, Forrest, visiting the places pertinent to Margaret's life. Through Donna's arrangements I had the pleasure of having tea with another Margaret Wilson at her home in Moncrief. This Margaret is a direct descendant of Margaret Wilson's Glenvernoch family.

Before and after my visit to Wigtown, Donna patiently answered a myriad of questions for me via e-mail. If I have drawn erroneous conclusions in re-creating Margaret's life, the fault lies in my not asking the right questions.

My American encouragers in the project include my critique group: Jean Capron, Jeanne Converse, Judyann Grant, and Aline Newman. Celia Livingston and the staff at the Melvil Dewey Library of Jefferson Community College in Watertown, New York, secured for me dozens of resources through Information Delivery Services. Kristi Holl, Nancy Morrison, Nellie Mae Schauer, and Liz Curtis Higgs helped me bring Margaret's story to life.

My manuscript was greatly enhanced by the editorial wand of Ranelda Hunsicker, who smoothed out the rough spots and spiced up the dull ones, while encouraging me every step of the way.

My greatest support came from my husband, Arthur, who has enriched my days and encouraged me in my writing life for forty years.

Who's Who
in the Story

Margaret Wilson: courageous Covenanter of Glenvernoch in Galloway, Scotland

Thomas Wilson: Margaret's younger brother

Agnes Wilson: Margaret's younger sister

John and Robert Wilson: Margaret's older brothers

Gilbert Wilson: Margaret's father

Janet Wilson: Margaret's mother

Fergus and Finlay Walker: neighbors of the Wilson family

Samuel Wilson: Margaret's uncle

Andrew and Gavin Wilson: Margaret's cousins

Margaret M'Lauchlan: Margaret's sixty-three-year-old friend and a staunch Covenanter

James Colquhoun: unpopular minister at Penninghame Kirk, where the Wilsons attended

Lady Stewart: wife of the laird who owns the land the Wilsons farm

Hugh M'Kail: young Covenanter preacher

Donald Cargill: Covenanter preacher who encouraged militant action

James Renwick: young Covenanter preacher who followed in Cargill's footsteps

Andrew Symson: minister at Kirkinner Kirk

Robert Grierson of Lagg: fierce persecutor of the Covenanters

John Graham of Claverhouse: fierce persecutor of the Covenanters

Laurie of Maxwelton: a bloodthirsty associate of Claverhouse and Lagg

Patrick Stewart: a magistrate in Wigtown

Provost William Coltrane: the chief magistrate in Wigtown

William Moir: clerk of Wigtown

I

EAVESDROPPING

Margaret swallowed hard and swiped angrily at the tears splashing her cheeks as she headed to the byre for the evening milking. If only she could stop imagining what it was like. Finlay striding across the moor toward Minnigaff on a mission of mercy to help some harassed Covenanter. Then the English dragoon thundering up on his horse, sword drawn, ears deaf to Finlay's shouts of innocence. The sword slashing through the air and into her friend's body. And for what? He wasn't headed to one of the forbidden believers' meetings as the soldier had assumed.

She felt like part of her had died with Finlay. And what must his twin brother, Fergus, be feeling? Finlay and Fergus Walker were her nearest neighbors and her best friends. Her grief doubled at the thought of Fergus's pain. Fear snaked around her heart as she considered the danger surrounding him and her older brothers, John and Robert. They were bold in speaking out for the right to keep the covenant they'd made with the Lord. Her brother Thomas was ten, two years younger than she, and her sister Agnes was only seven . . . safe for the time being from the perils the older boys faced.

God, we are all your children, Margaret prayed silently. *Please make the killing stop.*

If only life could be the way her parents said it once was, when attending kirk services was a delight rather than a royal command. Then, devout ministers preached God's Word without fear. But ever since His Royal Highness—she refused to call King Charles II by name—claimed to be the head of the Church of Scotland, everyone had to listen to ministers appointed by the bishops. Their messages were short on Scripture and long on haranguing anyone who opposed the king's interference with the kirk. Dissatisfied Covenanters who crept off to secret services led by true Presbyterian ministers risked punishment, even death.

As she pulled her milking stool close to the first cow, Margaret recalled the proud day when she stood with her parents to make a solemn covenant. There, before the Mercat Cross, she had raised her hand, pledging to recognize Jesus Christ as head of the church. Even then, savage dragoons, encouraged by His Royal Highness, oppressed the Covenanters. They hadn't yet bothered her family, but it was an uneasy peace.

Darkness was still three hours away when Margaret finished her evening chores. She decided to thread her way across the moor to her secret place. Her refuge was a hidey hole under a moss-hag about a mile from her Glenvernoch home.

She skirted the clumps of yellow gorse scenting the evening air with their sweet, nutty fragrance. Her thoughts flitted back one year to the day she had discovered this special spot. When she told her brothers about it, John chuckled.

"Robert and I go there with Fergus and Finlay to hide from you," he said. "We're surprised you didn't find it sooner." He winked at his brother. "Now we'll have to find another place."

Her memories took wings as Margaret neared her hidey hole. Voices! She crept closer, careful not to step on a clump of dried peat or to trip over the rough turf. Her heart pulsated in her throat as she recognized the voices—her brothers arguing with Fergus!

She tiptoed closer, knelt down, and placed her ear against the moss. Now she could catch most every word.

"Come with us, Fergus . . . deliver Father's message to Uncle Samuel . . . attend the conventicle . . . our cousins Andrew and Gavin . . ."

"You must not go to the conventicle!" Fergus sounded agitated but firm. "Those services are forbidden. You could get killed just for being there!"

"We know that," John answered, "but we're sick of being forced to accept something we don't believe."

"Don't you long to hear a real sermon?" Robert asked.

"Aye," Fergus said, "but what if we were reported?" He paused and then whispered hoarsely, "Remember Finlay." A longer pause. "Is it worth risking our lives—and exposing our families to danger?"

At the mention of Finlay, tears prickled Margaret's eyes.

"All the more reason to stand against King Charles. We need to support those who gather for the open-air meetings," Robert insisted.

"It's true Claverhouse and his dragoons attack without warning," John added. "They give no quarter to anyone. If we go," his voice softened, "we might not come back."

Margaret drew in a big breath and then had trouble pushing it out. Why was Father sending her brothers to Loudon

Hill at the same time a large conventicle was being held there? Didn't he know about the meeting?

The past year she had attended small, secret meetings with her brothers and the Walker twins. How it would warm her heart to be with hundreds of people at a large one! If her brothers were going to Loudon Hill, she must find a way to go, too. She'd ridden there once with Father. *It would be a long walk with the boys, but I could do it*, she reassured herself.

Margaret leaned closer to the moss-hag, cautious not to catch her foot in the heather.

"We must not tell Father about the conventicle." That was Robert's voice.

Ah. So Father didn't know. Sometimes he distanced himself from the struggles with the king. But more than once, after she had climbed the ladder to the loft, she'd heard him and Mother discussing the situation.

"I have a large family to feed," he'd said. "I just can't ignore the king's wishes. If we keep attending kirk, we should be able to hold on to the farm and our Galloway cows."

"Why doesn't King Charles leave our kirk alone?" Mother had responded. "I could forgive his other faults, if he'd stop this 'divine right' nonsense."

Margaret came back to the present with a jolt when she heard her name.

"We must not tell Margaret about the meeting," John said. "If she knows, she'll insist on coming with us. You know how she pesters."

"Why can't we take her?" Robert asked. "I'm sure she'd like to go."

"Too dangerous," John said. "It's hard enough to keep our local meetings a secret. It'll be more difficult to hold a large conventicle without the dragoons finding us."

A deep silence followed, broken at last by Fergus's weary sigh. "I will go with you," he said. "But we must never take Margaret where she'd be in danger." His voice dropped to a choked whisper. "My brother was killed close to home. The risks will be higher going to Loudon Hill."

Margaret swallowed hard at Fergus's tender words. He was fifteen, and she fancied him a wee bit. If he should decide to go to Loudon Hill with her brothers, she simply must go along! *I'll find a way to get the boys to take me*, she promised herself. Her decision made, she eased away from the moss-hag and turned homeward.

As she walked, she pondered how to get her wish without admitting she'd eavesdropped. If she found no other way, she would follow the boys when they headed out to take Father's message to Uncle Samuel. She'd lag behind until they were so far from home they wouldn't dare send her back alone.

Exciting things would surely happen at the conventicle in Loudon Hill. She intended to be present when they did.

2

THWARTED PLANS

Margaret tried to stay calm as John and Robert made their final plans for an early-morning departure to Loudon Hill. She had stowed a few things in a small sack to take along when she sneaked out behind the boys.

Father's prize cows had delivered more spring heifers than he could keep. Many a farmer would like to buy them, but he was offering them first to his brother Samuel.

"Tell Uncle Samuel he can have all that I don't need," Father said. "We'll hold them until he comes for them."

"What if he doesn't want them?" Robert asked.

"He'll want them," Father said. "Each spring he's been asking for some of my strong Galloways." He stood and stretched. "You have a long journey ahead of you, so you'd better say goodnight. Enjoy the Lord's Day with Uncle Samuel and the boys." He opened his mouth as if to say something more but shut it abruptly. He cast a hasty glance at Mother and then added, "We'll pray for you to have a pleasant walk and a safe return on Wednesday afternoon."

Margaret's heart flipped joyously at the thought of trailing her brothers to Loudon Hill. After exchanging quick goodnights, she scurried up the ladder to the loft she shared with her younger sister, Agnes. Just as she reached the top rung, her foot slipped. She gasped in pain as she landed in a heap at the bottom of the ladder with her right leg twisted under her body.

Father carried her to the bench by the hearth. Mother checked her leg with her comforting hands. "Thank you, Lord, it's not broken," she murmured. "Your ankle is badly bruised," she said. She rose to get a poultice of shepherd's purse to rub on it.

"There. That should help," she said, "but you'll have to favor it for a few days."

Mother's words broke the dam holding back Margaret's tears. She would not be following the boys to Loudon Hill in the morning. Father carried her up the ladder to her bed.

The next two days dragged on for Margaret since she and Agnes couldn't venture far. "I'll do the milking until your ankle is better," Mother said.

After breakfast, the girls ambled out to spend the morning watching the spring lambs. Agnes began plying Margaret with questions as they sat down on the grass. By the time they returned to the house, Margaret had explained why King Charles was upset with the Covenanters in southwest Scotland.

"His Royal Highness believes he is head of our church as well as of our government," Margaret said.

Agnes giggled. "When you say that, Meggie, you mean His Royal *Lowness*, don't you?"

Margaret smirked. "Aye! He insists we accept the English way of worship with him as head of the church."

"But we believe Jesus is the head of the kirk," Agnes chimed in.

Margaret sighed. "Years ago our kirk chose its ministers without the king poking his nose into our affairs." She raised her eyebrows and drew in a deep breath. "Now His Royal Highness appoints them and makes us attend kirk. He punishes anyone who worships elsewhere."

"Like the secret prayer meetings?" asked Agnes.

"Aye, and the conventicles, too," Margaret added, thinking of John and Robert.

Since it took several hours to walk to kirk in Penninghame parish, Margaret remained home on Sunday. "I'll stay with you," Mother said. They read some Scriptures and prayed together. Margaret bit her tongue to avoid revealing her thwarted plans. The morning dragged by as she thought about the boys at Loudon Hill. *What if dragoons attacked the conventicle?* she worried. *Fergus and her brothers could be killed.*

Sunday evening Father picked up his Geneva Bible, and the family gathered about him for their devotional time. After reading a long passage aloud, he explained it and then quizzed his children to make sure they understood it. When they knelt together, he prayed for John and Robert. His voice grew faint, but Margaret was sure she heard him whisper, "Forgive me if I was wrong in sending them to Loudon Hill at this time."

No one wanted to talk after Father ended his prayer. Though it was early to be retiring, they said their goodnights and went to their beds. As Margaret eased herself under the blanket with Agnes, she thought about Father's prayer. *He must know about the conventicle,* she thought. *Did he send John and Robert to Loudon Hill so they could attend the forbidden meeting? They will return on Wednesday if all goes well. If it doesn't . . .*

She was too worried to shut her eyes. *How would we find out if dragoons attacked the conventicle?* She buried her head and wept into her pillow. When she finally fell asleep, she dreamed that dragoons had attacked the forbidden meeting and Fergus and her brothers lay dying where they had fallen. She awakened sobbing from the nightmare.

Time stood still on Monday. A cloud of concern hung heavy over the farmhouse, though no one admitted being worried about the boys. Mother went about her work with sealed lips, and Father retreated to the fields. Margaret limped around, but she couldn't walk far. Thomas and Agnes were quieter than usual. At supper time, they ate their kail and oatcakes with scarcely a word spoken by anyone.

After eating, the family prayed together for John's and Robert's safe return. Father went out to check the cattle. When he returned, he and Mother retired for the night. Thomas and the girls decided to do the same.

Margaret crept up the ladder behind Agnes. Lying in bed, she stared up at the thatched roof, still thinking about John and Robert—and Fergus. "The boys should be halfway home by now," she said. "They could return in two days, but Father told them to take their time." She imagined them loping along over the moors in good spirits. "I wish I could have gone with them." She gave her sister a goodnight hug and shut her eyes.

As if by invitation, the nightmare of the previous evening returned. Margaret shivered and pulled the blanket closer to her chin. She tried to picture pleasant things in her mind. But the silence in the dark loft surrounded her like an evil presence. She kept her eyes closed—until she heard muffled footfalls outside.

No one traveled the moorland at night except in an emergency. A friend in need would call out. Whoever was approaching the house didn't want to be heard. The steps were louder now. *Was it a dragoon? Oh, Jesus, please, don't let it be a dragoon.*

Leaping from the bed, she ignored the stab of pain in her ankle and hurried down the ladder. She scrambled across the room and knocked on the door where her parents slept. "Father! Wake up! Someone is coming!"

Father slipped out into the room as the handle on the door clinked softly. Someone was testing it to see if the bolt was in place. "God save us," he mumbled as he grabbed his peat spade and stood back from the door.

3

CONVENTICLE
REPORT

Ever so slowly the door opened and three shadowy fig-
ures slid into the room as a chill chased up Margaret's spine.
Silence. Then Father gasped. His peat spade thudded to
the floor.

"May God be praised! The boys are home!" he said. He
encircled them within his strong arms. Margaret and her
mother swept into the room, followed by a sleepy Thomas.
Fergus seized Margaret's hands and drew her close while
Father lit the candles.

Mother bustled about preparing to feed the boys, but all
they wanted to do was sleep. Too weary to go one step farther,
they stretched out near the fireplace.

"God bless you, my sons," Father said, as he laid a hand
on the shoulders of each one. "Sleep well."

The next morning Margaret crept down the ladder at
her usual time. Mother was preparing a welcome home
breakfast.

"I can milk this morning," Margaret insisted.

Mother looked at her ankle and then at the food she was preparing. "All right," she said, "but leave the milk for one of the boys to carry back to the house."

Margaret tiptoed around the sleepers and headed out to the byre. As she finished milking the last cow, Fergus appeared and picked up the pail.

Mother placed a chair for Fergus next to Margaret at the breakfast table. Already flustered by his nearness, Margaret fidgeted, waiting to find out what happened at Loudon Hill. She pressed her forearms against her rib cage to calm the swirling uneasiness in her stomach. *When will this meal end?* she wondered as she pushed the food around her plate, unaware of what her mother had served.

Finally Father laid down his spoon, looked at the boys, and said, "We're happy you're home. We didn't expect you until this afternoon."

John shot a look at his brother and then began. "When we got to Uncle Samuel's house, he invited us to go to the conventicle. To hear Thomas Douglas speak."

"I wish I had been with you," Margaret said.

Father spun around to face her. "Thank God you weren't! Those services are illegal—and dangerous." He grimaced. "Besides, we're obliged to attend kirk."

Margaret was not about to drop the matter. "Aye," she said, "but I wish our minister spent more time teaching the Scriptures and less time scolding us." She looked at her brothers. "Did you hear a good sermon from Mr. Douglas?"

"May the day come soon when we can all hear good sermons," Father said. He turned his attention back to the boys. "What did you learn from the sermon, John?"

John frowned and shoved the hair out of his eyes. "Mr. Douglas was just beginning his sermon when a warning shot rang out," he said. "Claverhouse and some dragoons were headed our way."

Claverhouse! Torturer of the Covenanters! The mere mention of his name chilled like icy fingers. Mother gasped, and her hands flew to her head as if blocking out what she had just heard. Margaret stopped breathing. Terrified, Agnes began to cry and fled to her mother's arms.

Father blanched, his eyes wide with fear. "What happened?"

"Most of the men had come to the conventicle armed," John said. "Some had guns or pikes. Others carried pitchforks and clubs. Or cleeks grabbed from the fireplace. Uncle Samuel and Andrew and Gavin drew up in battle formation with the other armed men. The rest of us moved to the rear."

John stopped for breath, and Robert picked up the story. "Our men swarmed down to the high side of the peat bog. 'Twas near the farm of Drumclog. A few rode horses, but most were on foot. Whenever Claverhouse ordered his men to shoot, our men dropped to the ground. After the bullets whistled over their heads, they popped up and fired back. We were gaining the battle, so Claverhouse ordered his dragoons to charge."

"Their horses got stuck in a patch of mossy ground," John said. "We attacked them on foot. That sent them scurrying. One of our men stabbed Claverhouse's horse with his pitchfork."

Margaret watched the sparkle in her brothers' eyes as they relived the excitement at the confrontation. She wished she had been there with them. Just wait until next time. She'd

25

convince her brothers to take her along—without telling Mother and Father.

Father cleared his throat and began speaking in the harsh voice he used when he was terribly upset. "Claverhouse lost one of his dragoons who attacked a conventicle at Lesmahagow. No doubt he was seeking revenge at Drumclog." He inhaled deeply and stared straight into the eyes of his sons. His shoulders heaved upward and then settled back in place. "Now he's lost another battle—and his reputation." He sighed. "You can be sure he'll respond with more vicious attacks."

Robert's eyes brightened. "When he does, I want to be there to do my part."

"So do I!" John added.

Father screwed his face into a look of anguish. "Violence begets violence," he said in a voice so low they strained to hear him. "We must find a peaceful way to end this conflict."

"We've tried to do that for years," Robert said. "Still the king forces us to accept his style of worship. When we disobey, his dragoons hound us until we give in. Or kill us on the spot." A frown crept across his forehead. "We have to break his hold over our kirk."

"I'm not saying we should do nothing," Father said. "I dislike the king's interfering with our worship, but we won't change his mind by brute force."

Mother sighed. "I wish it weren't so hard to obey him."

"It's not that hard to attend kirk services," Father added.

Margaret sputtered. "We'd learn more if we stayed home and read the Bible ourselves."

Father looked at her and spoke gently. "I know it's frustrating for you when the minister launches into his tirades."

He looked at his sons. "I've begged the Lord for wisdom to know what to do. By attending kirk, I am protecting our livestock and our property."

"But, Father," Robert said, "you pledged to accept Jesus as head of the kirk. Even Charles swore the covenants before he became our king."

"Aye, and because he's broken them, he's lost claim to our allegiance," John added. "Because you attend kirk, you're criticized as forsaking the covenants."

"That's the price I must pay for my convictions," Father muttered.

Margaret's brow wrinkled. *Is Father turning the other cheek as Jesus taught us we should do?* she wondered.

She thought about kirk services. Mr. Colquhoun seemed more concerned with pleasing His Royal Highness than delivering a sermon to help his congregation grow in their love for the Lord.

Her father's words jerked her mind back to the problem at hand. "Mr. Colquhoun doesn't follow King Charles's edicts to the letter." He heaved another weary sigh. "So far he hasn't reported those who are absent from kirk. But if one of us is reported," he said, "that will draw attention to us. The dragoons could use it as an excuse to steal our beautiful cattle." He looked at the boys, his flinty eyes bright with warning. "I don't want you slipping off to attend another conventicle."

From out of the corner of her eye, Margaret watched Robert and John trade glances, and she read their minds. They would attend the next conventicle with or without Father's blessing. Would they take Fergus with them again? Probably. She hoped they'd take her, too.

"Father," Robert said, his voice full of respect, "we saw the skirmish at Drumclog, but we weren't part of it."

"No," Father replied, "but that doesn't mean you won't be remembered for being there." He stared briefly at one son and then the other. "If even one dragoon recalls your faces, he won't rest until he brings you down."

Margaret felt her lungs being squeezed tight inside her chest. She thought of Finlay. God forbid that the dragoons would remember her brothers or Fergus. But what if they did? What if they came knocking on the door tomorrow looking for them? Would they shoot them on the spot? Or would they drag them away to be hanged in the marketplace as a lesson to others?

4
VICTORY AT
DRUMCLOG

The week after John and Robert returned from Loudon Hill, Andrew and Gavin arrived bearing a letter from Uncle Samuel. Father gathered the family about the table to read it.

To my brother Gilbert,

The offer of your fine heifers tempts me to stay and fight for our cause. But I cannot. I was in the forefront of the skirmish at Drumclog. Having lost his brother, his horse, and his honor, Claverhouse will stop at nothing to even the score with us. By the time you receive this letter, I shall be safely across the sea in Ireland.

The men who led the fight at Drumclog praised the Lord for giving them the victory. In truth, the dragoons were outnumbered and outmaneuvered because they didn't know the terrain. Since that day the victors have pranced about the countryside raising men and arms. A confrontation is bound to come soon. May God have mercy on our men when they face this murderer again. He is sure to be backed by the English militia.

Ireland is the only safe place for my sons and me. Yet we cannot risk traveling together. Andrew and Gavin will join me after delivering this message to you.

If ever you must flee Glenvernoch, you and your family will find a haven in our new home across the sea.

I remain your brother in the faith,

Samuel Wilson
12 June 1679

Mother's eyes widened with the news that Samuel had fled. At the mention of Andrew and Gavin leaving Loudon Hill, she gasped. "I cannot bear it. We . . . may . . . never . . . see . . . you . . . again. May . . . the . . . Lord . . . protect . . . you." She buried her sobs in her apron.

John and Robert inhaled deeply. Margaret read in their eyes a longing to be directly involved in the struggle against His Royal Highness. How long would it be until they entangled themselves in open warfare against the king?

When Father finished the letter, silence thick as the fog from the sea that carried Uncle Samuel to safety overspread the room. Margaret stretched to relax the muscles that had cramped from Agnes leaning against her. Thomas looked wide-eyed at his cousins. The older boys exchanged glances that Margaret could not interpret.

Father's lips moved as if he was trying to speak, but nothing came out. Nor did anyone else respond for several moments. When Mother gained control of her emotions, she broke the silence. Looking at her nephews she said, "We'll miss you—and your father, too."

Father nodded toward Andrew and Gavin. "May God soon bring these troubled times to an end so you and your father can return to Loudon Hill."

"If God wills it, we will be back," Andrew said.

"Forgive me," Mother said, rising from her chair. "Come, girls. Andrew and Gavin must be hungry." Margaret and Agnes sprang up to help prepare the evening meal.

Father lit the candles at twilight. When the supper dishes were clean and the table scrubbed, Mother and the girls picked up their needlework and joined the others in front of the hearth. The talk soon centered on the plight of the Covenanters and the coming battle against the king's soldiers.

"Robert and I want to join the fight against Claverhouse," John said.

"Please, God, no!" Mother thrust her needlework aside.

Father spoke up. "King Charles considers us rebels because we disobey his laws." He took a deep breath. "So does God." Now all eyes were upon him. "When we rebel against our king, we bring judgment upon ourselves."

"But, Father," John began, "why must we submit to a godless ruler?" Margaret had asked herself the same question for many months.

Father squared his shoulders and swallowed a few times. "Violence is not the way to change things. Remember what happened to Moses after he killed the Egyptian. When we run ahead of God's plans, we make matters worse."

"Though we don't understand why, God is allowing King Charles to rule over us," Mother said. She picked up her needle and jabbed it into the linen. "Even though his behavior is ungodly," she added through gritted teeth.

Father closed his eyes for a moment. Then, speaking as if refreshed, he said, "We are in a hard place. God honors obedience. If we don't obey the king, our lives are in danger. If we do obey him, we're disobeying God. May God show us what to do before it is too late."

Mother raised her eyes to John. "Right now we Covenanters are divided. Your father is trying to change the situation from within the kirk. Those who take to the hills to worship do not agree with his stand. We can't both be right. I wish we could agree."

"We'll defeat ourselves by our divisions," Father said. "Only by working together will we find a solution to this dilemma. We must pray that God will change King Charles's mind. Or remove him from the throne." His voice lowered. "I wonder how many more of us must die before this happens."

Margaret's stomach lurched. This wasn't the first time Father had spoken of death. *To live is Christ. To die is gain.* But she wasn't ready to die, and she didn't want her family or her friends to die either. She fixed her glance on Father's face and saw a new commitment in his countenance. If need be, he would give his life in defense of the Covenanting faith. *Will my faith ever be as strong as Father's?* she wondered.

"That's why we need to join the resistance," Robert said. "To end this struggle once and for all."

Father's piercing glance focused on John and Robert. "You are too young to fight the dragoons. Besides, I need you here to help me with the cattle. I forbid you to get involved in any battles."

The boys slumped back in their seats, their faces mirroring their frustration. After several awkward minutes,

Mother spoke. "We've had enough talk about war. Let's speak of other things."

Andrew and Gavin stifled their yawns as they answered Mother's questions about Uncle Samuel and his decision to leave Loudon Hill. Before long they were bedded down near the hearth for their last night in Scotland.

A few days after the visit from Andrew and Gavin, Margaret returned from milking to find her parents in turmoil. John and Robert had slipped off to join the battle against Claverhouse. Mother clutched a short note they had left in their room. With trembling hands, she gave it to Father. Their eyes met briefly as he unfolded it. His voice faltered when he read it aloud.

> *To Father and Mother,*
>
> *We are going to Bothwell Bridge in place of Uncle Samuel and our cousins. Fergus will go with us. We must uphold the covenant even when it means disobeying you. If God gives us victory, we will return as soon as possible. If the battle is lost, know that we died for Christ's crown and covenant. Goodbye to you. And to Margaret, Thomas, and Agnes.*
>
> *Your sons,*
> *John and Robert*

Father's final words were barely audible as Mother's sobs filled the room. He reached out and drew her to his heart. Margaret felt a lump growing in her stomach. Struggling to hide her tears, she pulled Thomas and Agnes close. If only this dreadful war with His Royal Highness would end. Would they ever see their brothers again? And what if something happened to Fergus?

5

DISASTER AT BOTHWELL BRIDGE

After John and Robert left home, Margaret spent more time with Thomas and Agnes. When Thomas was busy helping Father with the cattle or in the fields, she and Agnes explored the moors.

"Come, Aggie," Margaret called one late summer morning when her sister was out with the lambs. "Let's go pick brambles." Margaret knew where the tastiest berries grew on their straggly, thorny branches along the meadows. She and Agnes headed out with their baskets and were soon picking the ripe fruit from their prickly stalks.

"You have purple lips, Meggie," Agnes said with a giggle.

"So do you." Margaret popped another juicy berry into her mouth. "Mother fancies brambles. Wait until she sees these giants."

The girls headed home with their brimming baskets.

When they reached the house, it was lunch time. "Look at these brambles," said Agnes, leading the way inside.

"We had a good time picking the—" Margaret stopped mid-sentence. There stood Fergus wiping sweat from his brow. Margaret's breath caught at the sight of his flushed face and his anxious eyes. She wanted to rush to him and hold him close, but she had to wait her turn. Mother and then Father hugged him with the warmth they'd been storing up for John and Robert. But why had he returned alone?

Margaret read in her father's eyes the question she was afraid to ask. Why hadn't John and Robert come home with Fergus?

Fergus spoke softly. "About five thousand Covenanters gathered near the River Clyde," he said. "We were sure God was on our side. We waited for instructions, but nobody told us what to do." He shoved his right hand through his hair as if stalling. "Our leaders argued for two weeks over who was fit to fight for the crown and covenant. Meanwhile the king's soldiers geared up for battle. Under the Duke of Monmouth and Claverhouse!" He shook his head and frowned. Margaret's mother twisted the hem of her apron, and her father looked grief-stricken.

"We were disorganized. Outnumbered three to one and facing the king's well-trained men. By the grace of God, we held our position—until we ran out of ammunition. The men who had swords charged, but we were no match for the king's army. Our horses stampeded. Our men fled the field with Claverhouse and Monmouth in pursuit."

Fergus paused as if searching for the right words to continue. "I came home by way of Edinburgh," he said softly. "There I learned the outcome of the battle." He blinked several times and then continued. "We lost only fifteen men in the struggle—but at least four hundred were slaughtered trying to get away."

"And what of John and Robert?" Father asked. "What happened to my sons?"

Margaret's heart raced. *Why doesn't Fergus tell us?*

"Our men panicked," Fergus said. "Many of them ran. The others surrendered. They were forced to lie flat on the ground all night. The next day they were marched back to Edinburgh. There was no place large enough to hold so many prisoners, so they locked them up inside Greyfriar's Kirkyard and th—"

"Get to the point, lad," Father demanded. "Did John and Robert escape?"

Fergus looked into Mr. Wilson's face. "The three of us fought until our ammunition was gone. Then, since none of us carried a sword, we scrambled away from the battlefield." Again Fergus fell silent, his eyes glassy from shock, his face haggard.

Please tell us what happened to my brothers, Margaret wanted to scream.

Fergus rubbed his forehead and continued. "When we got away from the battlefield, John and Robert decided to run off to Ireland before the soldiers rounded up escapees. They urged me to go with them." He looked at Margaret. "I couldn't do that."

An anguished cry erupted from Mother's throat. Father enfolded her in his arms, and the two wept silently. Margaret gathered Thomas and Agnes close, shut her eyes, and tried to keep her sobs inside. As she struggled to be strong for their sake, she felt a firm but gentle hand on her shoulder. She raised her head and looked into Fergus's tender eyes. Fergus brushed her forehead with gentle lips.

When the sobbing ceased, Fergus spoke again. "I promised John and Robert I'd return to tell you what happened."

"Weren't you afraid to come back, especially after Finlay was . . ." Father left his sentence unfinished.

"Yes," Fergus said, looking into Margaret's eyes. "I was afraid . . ."

"Thank you, Fergus," Father said. "God grant that John and Robert are safe with Samuel. May he bless you for returning."

Margaret missed her brothers, and so did Fergus. He visited Glenvernoch as often as he could to help fill the gap left in the hearts of the grieving family. He and Margaret grew ever closer, and he became a substitute big brother to Thomas. At kirk, he moved his stool to the aisle across from where Margaret sat. Then he invited Thomas to sit in Robert's former spot on his right.

One afternoon, Fergus showed Thomas how to make a whistle from a rowan branch. Thomas gave his new whistle to Agnes, and Fergus gave his to Margaret. Another day they made peashooters from hemlock. "These dried rowan berries make great ammunition," Thomas said, taking aim at a nearby gorse bush.

As time passed, an anxious semblance of normalcy settled on the Wilson home. Father did not share his grief over his sons' departure outwardly, but Margaret sensed his inner turmoil. "Never have I refused to accept King Charles as our civil leader," he said one evening as he gathered his family for devotions. "But now I'm having second thoughts." He thumbed the pages of his Bible until he found the passage he was seeking.

"Pharaoh persecuted God's people, just like King Charles persecutes us." He paused as if trying to make up his mind about something. "The persecution got so bad that God chose Moses to deliver his people."

"I wish God would send us a Moses," Mother said.

Father nodded. "Until he does, we have to obey our king, just as the Israelites were forced to obey Pharaoh." His brow wrinkled. "I resent being ruled by bishops. But until God shows us how to throw off their authority, we have no choice."

Margaret didn't agree. "Obeying the king forces us to go against our consciences. What good does that do?"

"It helps keep the peace," Father said. "The dragoons have not taken our cattle. Or destroyed our crops. They've not quartered themselves in our home." His eyes narrowed, and a frown creased his forehead. "By holding onto our farm, we have food to share with those who have lost theirs to the greedy dragoons."

"Your father wants change to come through peaceful ways," Mother said. "Meanwhile we help supply the needs of others."

That night Margaret lay in bed pondering Father's reasoning. *Is God really using him to save his people like he used Moses?* That was a comforting thought. *But what if Father's confidence is misplaced?*

6

ALARMING NEWS

Margaret shuffled into the kirk and sat down on her stool across from Fergus. She wished Mr. Colquhoun would stick to the Scriptures rather than complaining about the Covenanters so much. But at least she got to see Fergus each Lord's Day. She'd like it better if they could sit together, but women and men sat on opposite sides. Her heart did a snappy somersault when she looked at him. They exchanged smiles amid what sounded like the droning of a swarm of bees. Margaret leaned over and whispered, "What is everyone talking about?"

The buzzing halted abruptly as Mr. Colquhoun mounted the pulpit with less decorum than usual. Casting aside the gathering hymn and the prescribed opening prayers, he began the service in an angry voice.

"Barmy murderers! Were they honoring God by killing an unarmed man?" He scowled at the congregation as though they were to blame. "Those rebels will pay dearly for slaying Archbishop Sharp!" he bellowed.

Slaying the archbishop? A collective gasp filled the kirk. Anguished groans followed as the minister related how he had been attacked at Magus Moor. "Half a dozen of your *friends*," he sneered, "murdered him in front of his daughter on his way to St. Andrews." His eyes narrowed as he drew in a huge breath. "They told him he must die because he was responsible for the deaths of many Covenanters."

The minister spat out a list of offenses that his Penninghame parish knew nothing about. "Making trouble at Rutherglen! Putting out bonfires honoring King Charles on his birthday! Burning copies of the edicts against their behavior! Nailing their declaration to the Mercat Cross!" He snorted. "From Magus Moor to Drumclog, they have scorned our worthy king! But," he said smugly, "the score was settled at Bothwell Bridge! Where is their boasting now?"

Margaret's stomach knotted. With even more trouble sure to come, she needed to talk with Fergus.

The service finally ended. Fergus reached for her hand as the shocked congregation filed out quietly. Not until they were beyond earshot of the minister dared they speak openly. Margaret and Thomas huddled with Fergus and other young people while Father joined a group of men who lingered to talk. About fifteen minutes later, the families reunited to return home.

"The murder of Archbishop Sharp is unforgivable," Father said. "I abhor violence." He stared off into space as if he were expecting the answer to the Covenanters' dilemma to appear out of thin air. Then he added in a hushed voice, "Our men fought together at Drumclog, and God gave them the victory. But then he allowed them to suffer a grisly defeat at Bothwell Bridge." Silence reigned for a few moments. "When will they learn to follow the example of the Prince of Peace?"

A few days later Fergus invited Thomas to go fishing. They returned with six fresh trout. "Look what we caught," said Thomas. "With our bare hands!"

"You're making that up," said Margaret. He and Fergus liked to tease her.

"It's true," Fergus said. "It's called *guddling*. It's easy because there are so many fish." His eyes twinkled. "Would you like to learn to do it?"

Margaret nodded, and he continued, "You must be quiet so you don't scare the fish. I'll tell you how to do it. Then when we have time to try it, you can watch me." He settled back and began his explanation. "You flatten yourself on a ledge and breathe quietly. Then very slowly you slide your hand down into the water to find a fish." He wiggled his fingers as though he were searching under a ledge.

"Won't the fish be frightened if you touch it?" Margaret asked.

"It might," Fergus said. "But if it isn't, you tickle its back gently. Then you move your hand forward a tiny bit. If the fish stays in place, you reach underneath it and tickle its belly." He moved his hand slightly forward and backward. "This sort of puts the fish to sleep," he said. "When you reach the gills, you slip your fingertips inside them and hold onto your catch."

"It sounds easy," Margaret said. "I'd like to try it."

A week later Fergus took her to a deep burn flowing through a shady hillside. He nodded toward the ledge. "That's where we'll catch them," he whispered. "Watch me." They flattened themselves on the ledge. Very slowly he slid his hand into the water beneath it.

Margaret watched for a few minutes and then reached down toward the water. She gasped when her hand touched the cold surface. She hoped she hadn't scared the fish. She glanced at Fergus. She knew by the serene look on his face he was tickling a fish. *I want to do that, too.*

Very slowly she moved her fingertips in the water. *Ooooh. There it is.* She tickled her fingers slightly over the scales of the fish and concentrated on doing what Fergus had taught her. When the fish relaxed under her hand, she wanted to shout. Bit by bit she moved her hand forward until she reached the gills. The fish did not move. She held her breath, grasped the fish by the gills, and pulled it from the water.

I have guddled a trout! She held her trophy up for Fergus to see. Their eyes met over the fish for a brief moment—and then she loosened her hold on it. In a flash it was gone.

"I let mine go, too," he whispered, taking her hand and heading back to Glenvernoch.

7

MORE MILITANT
COVENANTERS

Early one autumn morning, Fergus greeted Margaret as she returned from milking the cows. "Let me carry the milk," he said as they walked back to the house. "My father and I have just returned from Edinburgh. I have more news about the prisoners from Bothwell Bridge."

Mother brought an extra plate and cup to the table and invited Fergus to join them for breakfast. Margaret slid closer to Agnes to make room for him on the bench.

"A few men escaped over the kirkyard fence," Fergus said in a strained voice. "Many more died of exposure. Or malnutrition."

Why didn't you rescue them, God? Margaret asked silently.

Fergus continued. "Some agreed to support the government— so they could go home and care for their families. The ministers who were captured were sent to prison at Bass Rock." Mother gasped. "A few men were brought to trial. And then hanged."

How dreadful, Margaret thought. *Thank you, Lord, for bringing Fergus home.*

Agnes grew pale as she listened to the fate of the prisoners. When Fergus mentioned the hangings, she squeezed her eyes shut and clapped her hands over her ears. Margaret put her arm around Agnes's shoulders and prayed she wouldn't have nightmares.

In early December, Fergus returned with more news. "King Charles has appointed his brother James to be High Commissioner to Scotland."

Father raised his hands to his head as if in pain. "God help us. He's the Duke of York, and he's more popish than his brother!" He shook his head. "Unless the Lord comes to our rescue, we'll never survive"

Margaret felt his despair, and her heart ached.

James assumed his duties in Edinburgh in 1680. Plans were afoot to welcome him to the castle by firing a royal salute from the monstrous cannon named *Mons Meg*. However, as the cannon thundered out its earsplitting salute, it burst its barrel. Having first been used to fire a royal salute to mark the marriage of Mary Queen of Scots to the Dauphin of France, *Mons* had now fired its last one.

When Fergus brought news to Glenvernoch of the explosive welcome, Margaret and Thomas burst into laughter. But Father did not appreciate the humor of the occasion. "That's a bad omen," he said.

Some of the Wilsons' neighbors wanted to fight King Charles's restrictions. Father tried to reason with them. "We're commanded to submit to our superiors, not to imitate their tactics. We must be willing to lay down our lives for Christ's crown and covenant." Those who could not agree with him fled to the hills—or to Ireland.

A few men of a militant persuasion seethed with discontent that they could no longer hold in check. Two of them were ministers, Donald Cargill and Richard Cameron. Fergus learned of Cargill's activities as he traveled about with his father bringing encouragement to Covenanters who had fled their homes. He spoke in awe of his hero.

"Mr. Cargill was left for dead at Bothwell Bridge, but he escaped to join Richard Cameron living in exile in the Netherlands. Within a year's time, the two returned to Scotland. Cargill preached at large conventicles, and the dragoons pursued him relentlessly." Fergus stopped to catch his breath. "Now there's a price on his head of three thousand merks—for opposing the restoration of Charles II to the throne!"

Father looked into Fergus's face. "Reverend Cargill fights for our convictions, but I disapprove of his firebrand tactics."

"Aye, but he's brave, and he furthers our cause," Fergus said.

Margaret noted the enthusiasm in Fergus's eyes and his hope of better things to come. She knew he'd be willing to give his life in defense of the Covenanters.

On July 22, 1680, Richard Cameron and his brother were killed in a fierce struggle with about 120 dragoons at Airds Moss. Though the Cameronian efforts died with them, feisty Donald Cargill snatched up their sword of resistance. Though the battle was lost at Airds Moss, the Covenanting cause was far from dead.

In September, Rev. Cargill excommunicated King Charles II and his brother James, Duke of York, at a large conventicle at Torwood. The king retaliated by raising the price on Cargill's head to five thousand merks. Anyone caught near his conventicles was to be hanged. Cargill eluded the bounty-hunting dragoons until the following summer. Then he was caught and tried before the Privy Council in Edinburgh. He was sentenced to death by a deciding vote cast by the Earl of Rothes, whom he had also excommunicated at Torwood.

Fergus and his father were in Edinburgh for a church council meeting on the day Cargill was hanged. "You should have seen how he died," Fergus said. "He forgave all the wrongs done to him. Then he asked the Lord to forgive the wrongs that any of the elect had done against him."

"What grace," Father said.

"At the foot of the scaffold, he sang a psalm." Fergus swallowed. "As he addressed the people gathered to witness his death, the drums drowned his voice. When he protested that he had no liberty to speak, the drums were silenced."

Margaret held her breath as Fergus continued. "Mr. Cargill assured us the Lord would return triumphantly to Scotland. He told us not to be discouraged." Margaret swallowed trying to contain her tears, but it didn't work.

Fergus blinked back tears, too, and then went on. "Mr. Cargill prayed privately for a wee bit. Then he mounted the scaffold saying, 'I go up this ladder with less fear than ever I entered the pulpit to preach.'"

A deathly silence filled the room. It was finally broken by Fergus's hushed voice. "After his execution, the authorities beheaded Mr. Cargill as a traitor." He lowered his head and swallowed several times. Then speaking in a voice so soft his words were barely audible, he added, "Mr. Cargill's head was fastened over one of the main gates into the city."

Margaret groaned aloud and fled to her room with Agnes in tow. "Dear God," she sobbed. "What is to become of us? I'm scared. For myself. My family. And for Fergus. Oh, Lord, please deliver us from men like Claverhouse and his dragoons."

8

THE TEST ACT

Gilbert Wilson handed his offering to the elder at the door as he and his family entered the kirk. Mr. Colquhoun entered at the second bell, wearing his usual black gown and bands—and his dour expression. He mounted the pulpit and bowed to the Laird and Lady Stewart in their box pew. Then, rather than calling the congregation to worship, he made an announcement.

"On August 31, Parliament decreed an oath called the Test," he said. "Henceforth anyone seeking public office must swear to accept the authority of King Charles over all matters, both secular and religious."

That said, he led the worshipers in a short opening prayer. The men doffed their hats but heard little of the prayer as they wrestled with yet another insufferable demand.

When the service ended, the people filed out silently, numbed by what they had been told.

"We're not officeholders," Father said on the way home, "so we won't have to take that abominable Test."

Supposedly the Test would be given only to men in public office. But when Fergus went to Minnigaff, he learned that agents like Claverhouse were forcing everyone to take it. "Some men have taken the oath to avoid further suffering," he reported to the Wilsons. "Others have sworn it because they're too exhausted to care anymore."

Fergus shoved his hair away from his face and said, "But many have refused the Test—and suffered the consequences." He looked hesitantly at Margaret and Agnes before continuing. "Three men were hanged in Glasgow. Their bodies were left to rot publicly. In Edinburgh, the tolbooth is full of Covenanters who refuse to swear the oath." His voice dropped a full octave. "Most of them will be hanged in the Grassmarket."

After a long silence, Thomas raised his head, and the edges of his mouth crimped a wee bit. "Even the children see it's foolish to force men and women to swear an oath they don't believe."

"What do you mean?" Margaret asked.

Fergus nodded to Thomas. "Go ahead and tell them what I told you."

Thomas began his tale. "The boys at Heriot's Hospital in Edinburgh decided to administer the Test to their watchdog since it holds 'a public office.' They tried to feed him a printed copy of the oath, but he refused it. They rubbed it with butter and offered it again. The dog licked the butter off but still wouldn't swallow it. As they were leading the dog away, a minister passing by asked where they were taking the dog. 'To be hanged,' one of them replied, 'for refusing the Test.' When the minister rebuked the boys, one of them responded, 'Then the dog is smarter than you are. He refused to swallow the Test that you accepted.'"

The Covenanters enjoyed some relief from persecution in December when the weather turned savage. Margaret shivered along with the rest of the family as they huddled around their peat fire. "Even the dragoons are forced to stay inside to keep warm," she said.

The family left the warmth of the hearth only to eat or care for the cattle. At night they rolled themselves in their woolen blankets and slept as close together as they could in front of the fire. Before hastening out to milk the cows, Margaret put on as many layers of clothing as she could wear and still move about. "The earth has turned to iron," said Father on returning from feeding the cattle. When Thomas went for water, he found the burn frozen solid.

One morning, Fergus appeared at their farmhouse to make sure they were not in need. Mother fixed him a warm drink. He unwrapped himself a bit from his woolen blanket and squeezed into the family huddle between Margaret and Agnes.

"Father and I have been taking food and blankets to the hill people holed up in drafty barns and sheds," he said. "They're cold, too, but they're grateful to be indoors—and for fires to keep them from freezing to death.

"Last week the laird discovered two servant lassies stealing kail from his garden," Fergus said. "He asked them why they didn't take the kail from one of the yards they'd passed before getting to his. When they said the other yards belonged to people as poor as they were, he let them off without punishment."

On a bit milder day in January, Father bundled up and walked over to Fergus's house to see if Mr. Walker had any news from around the area. He returned home in an agitated state. "Claverhouse has been appointed sheriff of Wigtown-shire," he said. "He's supposed to squelch our objections to the Test Act." He shuddered, but not from the cold this time. "If we refuse to give in, he'll quarter his soldiers in our homes. Plunder our houses. Eat up our provisions!"

In March, when Scotland began to thaw out, Claverhouse set in place his ruinous plans to force compliance with the Test Act. Margaret seethed as Mr. Colquhoun fawned over every move made by Claverhouse. Many a Lord's Day she wished she could speed up the hourglass attached to the pulpit and end the monotonous sermon.

After fidgeting through what felt like a two-hour tirade, Margaret complained to Fergus. He grinned at her and said, "That's how the Lord teaches us patience."

A few days later Fergus showed up at Glenvernoch. "Do you bring news?" Margaret asked.

"No news," he said. "I wondered if you might have time for a long walk."

Margaret darted inside to get her mother's approval. Fergus took her hand, and they headed down the path that led to the kirk.

"Why have you brought me here?" Margaret asked when they reached the kirkyard.

"You'll see in a minute." Fergus opened the kirk door and stepped back for her to enter. Taking her hand, he led her up to the pulpit where the hourglass hung on the edge. "If we take some sand out of this thing, Mr. Colquhoun won't speak so long."

He grinned as they set to work dismantling the time-keeper. "Next week's sermon will be shorter," Fergus said as they removed about one-third of the sand. He set the hourglass back in place and winked at Margaret. She giggled as they left the kirk, being careful to close the door behind them.

Margaret's heart sang as they retraced their steps to Glenvernoch. She couldn't wait to tell Thomas and Agnes what they had done.

Back at the farmhouse, Fergus stayed for a short visit with Thomas. Margaret overheard them discussing the heavy-handed tactics of the dragoons. "We need a leader who will fight back," Fergus said.

You're right about that, Margaret said to herself.

"Aye," said Thomas, "but Father says we must avoid violence at all costs."

No one at kirk complained about Mr. Colquhoun's shorter sermons. Margaret devised another plan to make the time more tolerable. She would concentrate on remembering every word Father had read from the Scriptures he had taught the family during the week. Occasionally she'd raise her eyes to the minister, but her thoughts were elsewhere. She especially liked Father's lessons about Moses and the Israelites. *We Covenanters have a lot in common with the Israelites when they were held in bondage by Pharaoh*, she told herself.

As these truths became a part of her life, she began to rethink her father's attitude toward kirk attendance. *I love Father. I respect his patience. But I have not inherited it.*

One Sunday morning, she squirmed on her stool as the minister's tirade against the Covenanters became insufferable. *Sitting here each Lord's Day, I'm obeying His Royal Highness. But by pretending to honor him, I'm breaking the covenant I made with Jesus,* thought Margaret. *Please, Lord, show me in your Word what you want me to do.*

9

MARGARET'S DECISION

While Margaret continued to search the Scriptures seeking the answer to her prayer, several seasons came and went. The Covenanters made it through the next winter by avoiding the dragoons. But spring brought sleepless nights to Margaret. Mr. Colquhoun's increasing bias set her teeth on edge. Claverhouse seemed to have doubled the number of intimidators determined to force everyone to take the Test. New rules were laid down by the Privy Council to squelch all resistance. Night after night she tossed on her bed trying to figure out how to keep her covenant—and her life.

Please, God, she begged while staring at the roof, *deliver us from having to take the Test.* Tears welled up in her eyes. *Comfort those who've been banished to the plantations for refusing it—and protect the rest of us.*

In September, Fergus brought exciting news. "Mr. Renwick has returned to carry the torch that had nearly burned out with Mr. Cargill's death."

Please, God, may it be so, Margaret prayed silently.

Across Scotland, Renwick's voice rang out like a trumpet, rekindling hope. But as he spread his extreme views, persecution increased. In October, many landowners were imprisoned until they took the Test—or bribed their way to freedom. Margaret grieved over the things Fergus told her and her family about the sufferings of the Covenanters who clung to their promises. Despite the painful persecution to which they were subjected, they refused to betray their friends. She shuddered and tried in vain to clear her mind of the atrocities.

At kirk, Margaret grew more disquieted. "I detest listening to Mr. Colquhoun each week," she complained to her father.

"I know you do," he said, "but at least we hear a brief message." He rubbed his forehead. "And we are obeying King Charles's command to be present."

"A pox on His Royal Highness," Margaret muttered. Then she spoke aloud. "Aye, a *brief* message. And then a spiteful complaint against us Covenanters." Defiance darkened her eyes as she asked, "How can we respect a drunken, immoral king?"

"We honor him because he is our king," Father said. "Not because of the life he leads."

"I understand how much you love us," Margaret said. "I know that's why you try to get along with the men sent to enforce the king's new laws. But it's wrong for them to bully us into submission."

No matter how much the dragoons threaten me, I will not give in to them, she vowed. But how could a lass of seventeen ever defend herself against an armed soldier determined to end her life?

I can never worship freely unless I join the Covenanters hiding out in the hills, Margaret reasoned. She had long admired those men and women who'd given up the comforts of home in defense of their faith. *That must have been difficult for them to do*, she reasoned. *But it's getting too dangerous to live out my faith at home. Still, I must consider my family.*

If she escaped to the hills, she'd be cut off from them. Forever. Tears threatened as she considered leaving. She loved Father and Mother, though she wished they'd take a stronger stand against the edicts of His Royal Highness. How could she leave Agnes and Thomas? Or Fergus. The thought of leaving him was too painful to consider. "Help me, Lord, to do what is right in your eyes," she prayed.

One afternoon, she pulled Father's Bible from the shelf, hoping for divine direction. As she read in First Corinthians, the apostle Paul's words about marriage spoke to her deeply. *"The unmarried woman careth for the things of the Lord, that she may be holy, both in body and in spirit."*

"That's what I want, Lord," she whispered and continued to the next verse. *"But she that is married, careth for the things of the world, how she may please her husband."*

Margaret closed the Bible and wandered off to her hidey hole for a long talk with the Lord. First, she prayed for Uncle Samuel, her cousins, and John and Robert. She prayed for her father and mother. For Thomas and Agnes. And for Fergus. Most of all she prayed that her life would count for Jesus—that he would keep her faithful to the covenant. *Please, Father, show me your will for my life.*

Warm thoughts of Fergus came tripping into her mind. *He's gentle, yet brave. He speaks up for truth and justice. He and his father often help the suffering Covenanters.* She sighed. *I like sitting near him at kirk—or wandering the moors.* She thought about the few innocent kisses they'd shared when alone. *I love Fergus, and I know he fancies me, but . . .* She paused, drew in a deep breath, and said aloud, "I willingly give him up to follow you, Jesus."

"Dear Lord," she prayed, "protect Fergus wherever he goes. I fancy him, Lord, but I give myself to you. I want to serve you with all my heart for all of my days." She thought about the loving relationship between her father and mother. For a fleeting moment she saw herself and Fergus in that same light. But her passion for God burned brighter than any dream of marriage. "Lord, I am yours. I choose to follow you and you alone wherever you lead me—whatever the cost."

She ended her prayer and sat quietly, reluctant to leave without some confirmation from the Lord. She had asked for wisdom, and she needed to know her next move. She recalled her father's words about the Israelites. "They endured bondage in Egypt until the Lord sent Moses to deliver them," he said. "We must be patient as they were."

Margaret pictured baby Moses being placed in his little basket in the River Nile when he could no longer be hidden. She thought about how the Lord had arranged for his mother to nurse him. As she envisioned him growing up in the palace, a new idea crept into her mind. *Moses' parents were brave enough to disobey Pharaoh and keep their baby hidden for three months. Later, the Lord chose him to lead the entire nation out of bondage in Egypt. So . . . there was a time when the Lord honored disobedience to the ruler.*

"Thank you, Lord," she whispered. She arose to return home.

Margaret slept well that night—and dreamed she stayed behind when her family set out for kirk. A few Sundays later, she decided it was time to act on that dream. But what would Father say?

10

REBELLIOUS DAUGHTER

The earthy aroma of burning peat wafted up from the thatched roof of the farmhouse as Margaret returned from milking early one Lord's Day morning. She handed the bucket of frothy milk to her mother and helped finish the breakfast preparations. Father and Thomas would be coming in shortly. She paused in front of the crude stone hearth where the fire burned with a lively flame. *It's cheerier than I am this morning*, she mused. She inhaled the woodsy peat reek, holding her breath as long as she could. Looking around the cozy room, she imprinted on her mind every precious thing that made her home a haven. It would be hard to leave behind the things she held so dear.

Father and Thomas entered, hung their homespun jackets on pegs by the door, and took their places at the table. Keeping her head low, Margaret slid onto the bench between her mother and Agnes, now thirteen and quick to notice everything she said and did. *It's a good thing Mother and Father can't read my mind*, she thought as she clasped her moist hands in her lap. She glanced at them and swallowed the lump growing in her throat. *I hope Mother will understand. Father will worry about the dragoons.*

Their breakfast of milk and day-old oatcakes ended, and Mother and Father went off to make their final preparations for attending kirk. Agnes chattered like a magpie as she and Margaret cleaned the plates and cups, but Margaret scarcely heard a word. *Never in my eighteen years have I questioned Father's authority. What will he say?*

She drew in a deep breath, pulled the family Bible from the sideboard, and sat down. Mother had taught her to read using the Bible, and Father regularly read and explained long passages to all his children. From childhood, she had learned to love God's Word and turn to it for direction. When Father strode into the room and saw her reading, his dark eyes widened.

"You can't attend kirk dressed like a milkmaid. You need to change your dress."

Margaret held her page with her index finger and looked up. "I'm not going," she said.

"Not going?" Father's eyebrows arched upward. "Are you ill?"

"No," she replied, shaking her head.

"Then hurry. We must leave soon."

Margaret reopened the Bible and began reading where she had left off.

"Margaret!" he bellowed. "You can't stay home!"

Margaret's heart battered her breastbone. She took a deep breath, closed the Bible, and looked up at the piercing eyes that pinned her to the bench. "Why should anybody attend kirk?" she said in a small, hard voice. She brushed some strands of auburn hair from her eyes and gulped to loosen the muscles tightening in her throat. "Sunday after Sunday we listen to

Mr. Colquhoun criticize us. He'd rather lick the boots of His Royal Highness than teach us the Scriptures. We learn more when you teach us."

Father's face clouded. His mouth opened and closed several times before any words came out. "You are my daughter. You will obey me. Now go!" He turned and stalked out to make a final check on the livestock.

Margaret opened the Bible again. Her brows knitted together as she tried to read. But the words skipped about on the page like lambs in springtime. She chewed the inside of her cheek and looked around the room as if searching for support for the decision she'd made. *Father expects me to be ready when he returns. What if he forces me to go?*

Father returned shortly. His brow furrowed when he saw she had not moved. "Margaret," he said through clenched teeth, "I told you . . ."

Margaret closed the Bible and stood up. Her heart pounded as she faced him. "Father," she said, struggling to keep her voice steady, "I have always obeyed you. Today I must obey my conscience."

She fought to dam the tears threatening to pour from her eyes. "For years I have sat in kirk each Lord's Day listening to the minister speak against us." Her words shot from her mouth like bullets. "He grovels to the lairds to keep his stipend, but he shows little love for the rest of us." She blinked to control her tears, but she could not hide her anguish. "Why doesn't God hear our prayers and deliver us from these false shepherds?"

Father's chin dropped in shock. He opened his mouth to speak, but Margaret wasn't finished.

"I pledged to honor Jesus as head of the kirk. You and Mother and the boys did the same. His Royal Highness cannot take the place of Jesus." She could no longer keep the tremor from her voice. "Jesus Christ is the spiritual head of the kirk in Scotland. Not His Royal Highness!"

The frown on her father's face deepened into a fierce scowl. "What you say is true. But the king demands that we attend kirk."

"He has no authority to do so!"

"He is our king. He is to be obeyed."

"Not when he contradicts the Scriptures," Margaret protested. "Our first obedience is to Jesus Christ."

A dark vein throbbed in Father's temple "You ken what happens to those who don't compear. We cannot risk losing our farm!"

As the pair argued, the rest of the family entered the room. Mother tugged anxiously at the strings of her linen mutch. Agnes clutched the hem of her woolen cloak and crept closer to Thomas.

Father opened his mouth, but no words came out. He tried a second time to speak. When no words came, he spun around and nodded to the others. "Come," he said, yanking his jacket from its peg. "We must be on our way."

At the door he paused and turned to Margaret. "We will discuss this matter when I return." He slapped his blue woolen bonnet onto his head and strode toward the door with the others in tow. "I pray the minister doesn't call the roll today," he mumbled as he went out.

Agnes gripped her brother's arm as she followed Father. Mother turned to Margaret with eyes confused, yet somehow supportive. She hesitated—and then left behind the others.

As the door closed after her, Margaret inhaled deeply. She wasn't worried about herself. But what might happen to her family if Mr. Colquhoun reported the absentees today? The thought grieved her, but her decision was made. *No matter what happens, I will not betray King Jesus.*

She looked down at Father's Bible still in her hands. If only she were taught the Scriptures regularly in the kirk. But she wasn't. The only way she could learn them was to slip off to secret Bible studies.

Her brow wrinkled, and she chewed her lower lip. *What would Father do if he thought I'd run away to join the hill people?* She drew in a big breath. *Thomas and Agnes would insist on leaving with me. Am I wrong to put them in danger?*

She straightened her shoulders and spoke aloud. "I will find a way to keep the covenant." She didn't know how she would manage that. It was too big a matter to settle now. Today she would study the Scriptures—at a forbidden Bible study at Fergus's home. It was a four-mile walk, and she must hurry. She wrapped her woolen cloak about her shoulders and stepped out into the brisk morning air. *Please, God, keep me safe.*

II

SECRET TRYST

Margaret breathed in the crisp air, grateful there was no snow to capture her footprints. Still, she must keep out of sight as much as possible. Dragoons often rode out on Sunday mornings hoping to catch Covenanters slipping off to secret services. Since she knew every inch of the moorland on the way to Fergus's home, she could melt into the hills as silently as the heather growing all around. As she hurried along thinking of him, she felt her cheeks glowing. Last Sunday at kirk Fergus had whispered to her, "We're holding a Bible study next Lord's Day in our barn." When she passed under a large rowan tree, a flock of lapwings swept over her head. "Pee-ee-wit, pee-ee-wit," they called. *That's strange*, she said to herself. *Lapwings usually fed in the winter stubbles at night and slept during the day.*

"Sorry, birds. I didn't mean to disturb you." She paused, enjoying them. Only God could create such shiny black and white feathers. She loved the stumpy, wispy crests on the younger birds. *I wonder if the hill folk see lapwings.* She hoped so. But now she must hurry.

Scurrying across a moss-hag, she slipped and fell. She cried out as pain shot through her ankle—the same ankle she'd bruised when she fell from the ladder. When she tried to stand, it ached worse. She was only halfway to Fergus's farm. Pain or no pain, she must keep going.

Hobbling along, she finally reached the cairn that marked the three-quarters spot. She leaned against the stones to rest her ankle. As she looked up from her feet, she spotted a lone helmeted horseman headed in her direction. "God, help me!"

She crept behind the cairn to hide. Her heart thudded in her ears as he directed his horse along the sheltered path she'd taken. She hoped he didn't know where the boggy sections were. Closer and closer he rode to the spot where she crouched, peering out at him. What if he discovered her?

She stopped breathing as the soldier approached the spot where she had slipped. Without warning, his horse lost his footing. One front foot dropped through the thin covering of moss and heather. Curses sullied the air. When at last the dragoon got the horse back on solid ground, he turned abruptly and galloped back the way he'd come.

Margaret pulled herself up, being careful to favor her injured ankle. Grimacing, she put her weight on it and took one small step and then another. Gritting her teeth, she limped along. *I must hurry. I've already missed some of the meeting.* At last the Walker steading came into view. She had only a few yards to go when several people left the barn. They scanned their surroundings and then melted into the moorland. Fergus appeared next, frowning. He spotted her struggling along and hastened to help her. "Margaret," he whispered hoarsely. "What happened?"

"I argued with Father about attending kirk," she said. She bit her lip. "That made me late leaving home. In my haste,

I slipped crossing the moss-hag near the cairn." She sniffed, trying not to cry.

Fergus placed an arm around her waist. "Let me help you into the house."

Leaning against his brawny shoulder, Margaret felt his heart thumping inside his chest. Something must have disturbed the gathering. "I'm sorry I missed the Bible study."

Fergus nodded as he helped her inside. While his mother bandaged her ankle, he explained what had happened. "Last week one of our friends overheard the dragoons boasting that they would soon catch me," he said. "They've been trying to do that for a long time." He stared across the room as if trying to see what lay ahead. "We had just begun our study when the lookout spotted a dragoon riding hard in our direction."

Margaret stiffened. "I saw him. His horse floundered where I had slipped."

"I hope he's not skulking about now," Fergus said, glancing down at Margaret's ankle. Fergus's mother inspected the bandage.

"That should keep the swelling down," she said. "It doesn't appear to be a severe sprain, but you need to favor it until it heals." She laid a comforting hand on Margaret's arm. "We can still have our study. Stay and have dinner with us." She glanced up at her son, who stood anxiously nearby. "Fergus can see that you get home safely this afternoon."

"Thank you, Mrs. Walker," Margaret said, trying to ignore her throbbing ankle.

Fergus's father led in prayer, they sang a psalm, and then he opened his Bible to Romans. "Recompense to no man evil for evil. Provide things honest in the sight of all men. If it be possible, as much as lieth in you, live peaceably with all men.

Dearly beloved, avenge not yourselves, but give place unto wrath: for it is written, Vengeance is mine; I will repay, saith the Lord."

Margaret hung on to every word as Mr. Walker explained the passage in his calm, reassuring voice. *How can we live peacefully with dragoons who hunt us down like mad dogs?* She knew some of the hill people carried weapons for self-defense. She fidgeted, waiting for the opportunity to speak. When Mr. Walker concluded his teaching, her words tumbled out. "Is it wrong for us to defend ourselves against the dragoons?"

Mr. Walker reopened his Bible. "Let me repeat something." He scanned the page to locate it. "If it be possible, as much as lieth in you, live peaceably with all men." He closed the book and looked back at her. "We are commanded to overcome evil with good," he said. "We cannot do that by shooting our enemies."

"But how can we live at peace when we are ruled by a godless king?"

"We search the Bible to learn the Lord's will in each situation." A deepening frown creased his brow. "It's not easy to own the covenant." He paused and added softly, "At times we must suffer here on earth. But Jesus is preparing us an eternal home in heaven."

Margaret nodded. Mr. Walker's words had confirmed the decision she'd been trying to make for several months. The hard part would be to tell her parents.

Fergus closed their study with a prayer. Then Mrs. Walker laid the table with the food she had prepared the previous day. Midway through the meal, Fergus turned to Margaret. "Father's right," he said. "It's not easy to own the covenant." He hesitated, measuring each word. "The dragoons have been searching for me for three years." He paused and then said softly, "I wanted to be one of the young men who stand guard when ministers like Cargill and Cameron speak at conventicles." He grimaced. "Now I must flee to save my life."

Margaret gulped and flung her hand over her breast. *Please, God, no!* If he left, she couldn't go with him. She belonged to Jesus—body, mind, and soul. She forced herself to breathe deeply to quiet the turmoil in her heart. The argument with Father. The reminder of her older brothers running for their lives. And now she might lose her best friend, too. *Oh, God, why don't you rescue us from His Royal Highness?*

Finally finding her voice, Margaret asked, "Why do the dragoons keep pursuing you?"

"They probably saw me with John and Robert at Bothwell Bridge. I've been hiding from them ever since." He gazed into her eyes. "Margaret, it's not safe for me to be seen anywhere."

Margaret's voice trembled. "You wouldn't leave Scotland, would you?"

Fergus shook his head. "No," he said, looking into her eyes.

Heaviness settled over her like dense fog arising from the Solway Firth. They finished their meal in silence until Margaret said, "I must get home before my family returns from kirk."

Fergus rose from the table and extended a hand to help her stand. "I'll see that you get there safely."

Margaret winced as she put her full weight on her ankle. "Thank you." She leaned on his protecting arm.

Fergus chose the main path to Glenvernoch. "It will be easier," he said, "and faster. Let's ask the Lord to protect us along our way."

12

DOUBLE TROUBLE

Margaret and Fergus had scarcely left the house when she spotted a horseman crossing the moors headed in their direction. "Look!" she gasped. Fergus tensed.

"God help us," Fergus said as the rider drew closer. "It's another dragoon."

"It's the same one I saw," Margaret whispered. "He's returned with a fresh horse."

"Halt!" the dragoon bellowed as he approached them.

Margaret refused to cower. *Does he think we're deaf? Or does he expect us to sprout wings and fly away?*

The dragoon glared down at them, his steely gray eyes piercing them like a sharp sword. "Whence and whither bound?" He shouted as though he were His Royal Highness's personal servant and they were scullery maids.

Before Fergus could respond, Margaret limped forward. "I twisted my ankle on the way to the services," she explained. "My friend is taking me home."

The dragoon looked from her to Fergus—then back. *He's memorizing what we look like*, Margaret thought. "Huh!" he snarled.

"See that you're both present next week." He turned his mount and rode off like a conquering hero.

"A pox on him!" Margaret muttered. Fergus drew her close, and she felt the beating of his heart match the thumping of hers.

"God is watching over us," he whispered. They hurried along as fast as Margaret's ankle allowed.

When they reached Glenvernoch, Fergus helped Margaret into the house. "I must not stay," he said. "If your family found me here, your father would be upset." Reaching down to take her hand, he whispered, "Margaret, you know I fancy you."

Margaret looked into his eyes, seeing the depth of love that had been growing there for years.

Fergus spoke rapidly. "Now that another dragoon has seen me face to face, he'll also be watching for me." He shook his head as if to shake away the enemy. "I'm moving to Drum-jargon to live with my uncle."

"Oh, my . . ." Margaret tried to keep her voice steady. "I will miss you . . ."

Fergus slid onto the bench beside her and took both her hands into his. "Margaret, please come with me. I want you with me always. Go with me, and become my wife."

Margaret's eyes widened. Her heart raced. She looked into his deep, brown eyes and tried to find the right words to tell him how much she loved him, but that she could not marry him.

As they gazed into each other's eyes, the door of the farmhouse opened. Father and Mother strode in, followed by Thomas and Agnes. Fergus blanched and dropped her hands.

Father stared at Fergus as if he were seeing a spirit. "What's going on here?" He waggled a finger at him. "You get out of here, and don't ever come back!"

"Please, Mr. Wilson, let me explain why I'm—"

"I *know* why you're here." He pointed an angry finger toward the door. "Go!"

Fergus gave Margaret a quick, anguished glance and then obeyed her father's order.

As the door closed behind him, Margaret's father turned to her. "I thought you stayed home to study the Bible!" He glowered at her. "Your behavior is a disgrace to our family."

"Father," Margaret said, struggling to keep her emotions under control, "let me tell you—"

"Haud yer wheesht!" He pointed toward the loft. "Go to your room," he said, stomping off to change his clothing. "I'll talk to you later!"

Margaret stood to obey him. The moment she put her weight on her sprained ankle, she cried out and crashed to the floor. Thomas sprang to her side.

Seeing Margaret's bandaged ankle, Mother rushed to gather her into her arms. "Lord, have mercy!" She turned to Thomas. "Help me get her back to the bench."

Agnes pulled her father's jacket from its peg and spread it out for a cushion.

"What happened to your ankle?" Mother asked.

Margaret bit her lip at the searing pain. Her mother held her gently while Agnes and Thomas hovered nearby. "I went to a Bible study at Fergus's house," she said and then related what had occurred on her way to the meeting. "Fergus helped me home," she explained. "We just got here." This was not the time to say that he'd asked her to escape to Drumjargon with him, especially when Father believed Fergus's behavior toward her had been improper.

Janet Wilson looked deep into her daughter's eyes. "I believe you, Margaret. I'm sorry you slipped on the way to the Bible study." She hesitated a few seconds and then added in a voice so low Margaret had to strain to hear her, "I wish my faith were as strong as yours."

And I wish it were strong enough that you would think for yourself, instead of echoing Father, Margaret said in her heart. Silence filled the space between them. Then her mother drew her close and whispered, "You must do what you feel is right—even when Father and I disagree with you." She nodded toward Thomas. "Your brother will help you up the ladder."

Agnes crept up after them.

When Margaret saw the tears clouding her sister's eyes, she wrapped her arms around her. "Things will turn out all right, Aggie."

"I'm sorry you twisted your ankle," Agnes said. "And I'm sorry you didn't get to the Bible study on time . . . and now Father is angry with you . . . and he's told Fergus never to come back . . . and . . ."

Margaret hugged her tighter. "Grown-ups don't mean to be cruel. Sometimes they just don't understand us." She paused, thinking of Fergus. "No matter what happens, we have each other. And we'll always have Jesus to help us."

Late in the afternoon, Margaret faced the dreaded discussion with her father. "Margaret," he called up the ladder. "I want to talk to you. Now!"

Thomas climbed up to the loft to help her down. "Sit there," Father said, pointing to the bench beside Mother. "I expect you to set an example for Thomas and Agnes," he said, "and to obey your parents." He glanced down at her bandaged ankle. "Perhaps the Lord has punished you for not attending kirk."

Margaret didn't believe that, and she doubted that he did. But what could she say in response?

Father's shoulders rose and then lowered as he heaved a sigh. He appeared to be struggling to find the words he wanted. She waited for him to speak. "At the close of the service this morning, Mr. Colquhoun called the roll," he said. "What do you think will happen when he reports you as absent?"

Margaret kept silent.

"Answer me!"

Margaret spoke softly. "I suppose Lagg or Claverhouse will send one of the dragoons to ask why I wasn't there."

"And what will you tell him?"

"I will tell him the truth," she said. Father stared at her as though she were a young child not comprehending the adult world. Yet she could see his eyes were clouding.

"Margaret," he said in a voice ready to spin out of control, "times are getting harder for us. We must not deliberately break the laws imposed upon us." He swallowed, gulped some air, and continued. "If Mr. Colquhoun reports that you did not compear, your life will be in danger, just like John's and Robert's." His voice quivered as he mentioned her brothers. "We've tried to protect you and Thomas and Agnes," he said. "We don't want to lose you, too."

Tears slid down Margaret's cheeks, but she said nothing.

"Return to kirk so the dragoons will leave us alone," her father pleaded. "If you don't, we can expect many troubles. Troops quartered on our farm. Our house spoiled. Our food devoured. Our livestock stolen." He caught his breath and added, "Your mother and Agnes will not be safe from their unholy advances." He looked directly into her eyes. "I could be fined for every service you miss." His lower lip quivered as he asked, "Don't you understand what might happen to us?"

Margaret swallowed several times trying to dislodge the lump growing in her throat. "Mr. Colquhoun is a mean-spirited minister. He *pretends* to follow every command of His Royal Highness, but he's never reported anyone." She grimaced and added, "Maybe he's just trying to frighten us." That's what she hoped, though she scarcely believed it herself.

Sensing her father's anxiety, Margaret spoke in a hushed voice. "All I want is to keep the covenant I made with Jesus." Looking kindly at him, she said, "Surely you remember the day I raised my hand to swear my loyalty to Jesus Christ." She breathed a silent prayer. "I refuse to honor a godless king," she said. "I *will* keep the promise I made." She stared long into her father's face and then added, "I want to slip away and join the hill folk."

Her mother's hands flew to her face. "Margaret!" she gasped. "Please don't talk of such a thing!"

Her father drew back as if she had struck him. "My child!" he said, struggling to keep his voice under control. "Have you taken leave of your senses? These are dangerous days!" His chin quivered as he struggled to speak. "If you run away, you cannot come home again. Ever! We will be forbidden even to speak your name." Burying his face in his hands, he moaned. "Is your faith strong enough to accept all that?"

"I pray it is," Margaret whispered. Inwardly she felt as unsettled as a storm-tossed boat on the North Sea, but she would trust the Lord to take away her fears.

"Consider it carefully, child," her father said. "Once you leave, you will be a fugitive. We will be forbidden to help you in any way. The dragoons will hound you until they track you down."

Margaret looked him in the eye. "I have already considered it," she said. "I must go."

"Then think about your family." His eyes begged her to change her mind. "Can you leave Thomas and Agnes knowing you may never see them again?"

Tears again welled up in Margaret's eyes. "I have thought about these things. And prayed about them for many days." She blinked and swallowed. "I love you, Father. I love Mother and Thomas and Agnes. But Jesus said, 'He who loves father and mother more than me is not worthy of me.'"

"You must change your mind!" Father said. He stared at her, shook his head, and left the room.

Margaret turned to her mother, "Please pray that the Lord will keep me safe."

Mrs. Wilson knelt with her children and prayed for each one by name.

"I love you, Mother," Margaret said, rising from her knees. She looked into the faces of Thomas and Agnes. "And I love both of you." *But I love Jesus most of all*, she said to herself.

13

A Visit to Castle Stewart

The events of the previous day cast a shadow over the new morning. The family ate their steaming bowls of porridge in silence. When they finished, Father and Thomas headed out to check the sheep. It would soon be lambing time, and they kept a close watch on the ewes. Agnes went outside to cast crumbs to the chickens pecking about in front of the byre while Margaret made the beds. A short time later, Thomas hurried up from the pasture carrying a newborn lamb.

"Aggie," he said, "this little one came early. It needs your help." He handed it to her and returned to the pasture.

Agnes wrapped her arms around the trembling creature and carried it to the house. "Mother," she said, "I've never seen such a wee one." She wrapped it in a woolen blanket and laid it near the hearth while she warmed some milk.

"Now, little one," she said, picking up the tiny bundle. "You must be hungry." She stuck her index finger into the milk and then into the lamb's mouth. Again and again she wet her finger in the milk and tried to get the lamb to suck it. She

tickled it under its tail to stimulate the sucking instinct—and
waited for the gentle licking to begin.

Mother watched Agnes care for the lamb. "If it will not
suck on its own, it must be too cold. Or too weak. You'd better get the whiskey."

Reluctantly Agnes laid the lamb down and went for the
only remedy she knew. When she returned, she picked up
the lamb and forced drops of whiskey into its tiny mouth. It
wouldn't take much to make it sleep. When it revived, she
would teach it to drink from a bowl. The lamb would live in
the house until it was big enough to run with the other spring
lambs in the pasture.

Meanwhile Mother turned back to her own household
chores. Today was her day to bake bannocks. She knelt by the
hearth coaxing heat from the burning peats.

"Was I the only one absent from kirk?" Margaret asked
as she laid more peats nearby.

"No, you weren't." Mother tucked some wayward wisps
of hair under her woolen mutch and stood up. "A dozen or
so were missing, including Lady Stewart—again. That could
make problems for her."

"Because she is the laird's wife?"

Mother nodded. "She's been absent quite a few Sundays.
If Mr. Colquhoun reports her, she'll be in big trouble."

"What will happen to her?"

"Claverhouse will probably threaten the laird. He'll
demand their attendance at kirk next week." She twisted her
apron as she talked. "I suppose Lady Stewart will be fined."

Margaret chewed her lower lip. "Maybe Lady Stewart is
ill." When her mother didn't respond, Margaret grew bolder.
"May Agnes and I go to Castle Stewart to find out?"

The silence sounded loud to Margaret as she waited her mother's reply. After what seemed a very long time, she responded in a voice that quivered slightly. "Lady Stewart risks everything she has to own the covenant." She looked into Margaret's eyes. "You're so like her." She hesitated again and then said softly, "She does what the Lord tells her, and so do you." She turned to give the peats a fierce jab. "I am afraid for her. The dragoons know she attends the conventicles. One of these days Mr. Colquhoun *will* list her as disorderly. Then the wretched soldiers will be sent to extract a fine for every Sunday she's been absent."

Mother shook her head and sighed. Her eyes held that far-off look that Margaret recognized each time she thought about John and Robert. "I don't want you girls to get into trouble because you visited her," she said. "I fear for your future. It's good that you think for yourself. That your faith is strong. But when you oppose the king . . ."

Margaret waited for her mother's wandering thoughts to return. When they did, she spoke softly. "Can you walk that far with your bad ankle?"

Margaret nodded. "It feels much better this morning. If we walk slowly, it will be all right."

"Then I give you leave, but take the hidden path."

Margaret embraced her mother. "Thank you," she whispered. "We'll be careful." She glanced at Agnes, who was holding the sleeping lamb. "Come, Agnes," she said. "We'll be back before your lamb wakes up."

The sisters made their way behind the farmhouse and past the kailyard to the path that led to the laird's castle. Margaret could see her breath in the brisk spring air as she stopped now and then to rest. When the old square towerhouse came into view, Lady Stewart was outside with her terriers.

"Whuff! Whuff! Whuff! Whuff!" The little white dogs barked out a friendly greeting.

"Good morning, lassies," Lady Stewart said. "You're far from home on a crisp morning. Come in."

Agnes looked up at the tall lady with the kind eyes and gentle voice. Though she was the laird's wife, she befriended the families of all the tenant farmers.

Lady Stewart glanced toward Margaret. "You're limping. What happened?"

"Aye," Margaret said. "I twisted my ankle yesterday. It's much better now."

Lady Stewart seated the girls near the blazing hearth and sat down at her spinning wheel opposite them. After dipping her slim fingers into a bowl of water nearby, she set the wheel to turning.

"We've been missing you at kirk," Agnes said. "Have you been sick?"

Lady Stewart shook her head and straightened her stays. "No," she said and then sighed.

"Yesterday at the end of the service Mr. Colquhoun called the roll," Agnes blurted out, her voice reflecting her fears for Lady Stewart.

Lady Stewart's dark eyes brightened, and the corners of her mouth twitched. "Was I the only one absent?"

"The Walkers weren't there, nor the McClures."

"I wasn't there either!" Margaret struggled to keep her emotions under control. "I used to enjoy hearing the bell call us to worship, but not anymore. I want more than the short lesson Mr. Colquhoun gives us each Sunday. I own the covenant," she said. "I don't want to go back to kirk." She blinked to hold her tears in check.

"There was a time when kirk attendance nourished our spirits," Lady Stewart said. "Now it's a political duty."

Margaret shoved her hair under her snood. "Father says His Royal Highness rules the kirk by divine right."

Lady Stewart grimaced. "That's what King Charles thinks." She spoke softly as she continued to spin. "If you refuse to attend kirk, you'll be declared a rebel and the dragoons will hunt you down." She looked up from her spinning into Margaret's eyes. "Once they find you, they are apt to kill you on the spot." Lady Stewart left her spinning wheel and gathered the upset sisters into her arms. "Your father wants to protect you from those murderers."

"I can't remember why our own ministers were turned out," said Agnes.

"King Charles insisted they be reappointed by his bishops." Lady Stewart frowned again. "To do so would be giving the king authority over the kirk. When they refused to do that, they were forbidden to preach."

"That didn't stop them, did it?" Margaret said.

"Nothing will silence them—except death. They'll preach wherever they find a congregation."

"Mr. Colquhoun doesn't like us Covenanters, does he?" Agnes asked.

Lady Stewart shook her head. "The king's ministers give their allegiance to him, not to any covenant they've made with the Lord. They seek his favor rather than studying the Scriptures so they can teach us. That's why I've been skipping the services." She paused and then added, "If you want to hear a real sermon, you need to attend a conventicle."

"I wish I could," Margaret said. She stared into space, straining to see the future. "I think I'd like to join the hill folk. Is it hard to survive on the moors?"

Agnes gasped, and her face paled, but Lady Stewart smiled at Margaret. "None of us survives on our own. We get our strength from the Lord."

Margaret unconsciously chewed the inside of her cheek. Catching herself at this annoying habit, she stopped and said, "I know Covenanters are abused when they are caught. What if the dragoons catch me?"

"Everyone who tries to live a godly life will be persecuted," Lady Stewart said. Margaret nodded. Some of her friends had been tortured by the king's soldiers. She wanted to be strong, but she trembled at the thought of facing the dragoons. "Each day I ask Jesus to protect me," Lady Stewart added. "I ask him to change the heart of King Charles—and of cruel men like Graham of Claverhouse and Grierson of Lagg."

At the mention of the dreadful persecutors, Margaret flinched and Agnes trembled. "Father says things would work out if we obeyed the laws of the land," Margaret said. Her brow wrinkled. "I worship King Jesus, not His Royal Highness."

"We must obey the king's rules when they agree with God's laws," Lady Stewart responded. "When they don't, we cannot obey them." She shook her head as if to shake away the unreasonable demands of King Charles. "Do you have a Psalter?"

"Aye," Margaret said. "Sometimes we sing in the evenings and always on Sunday afternoons. We sing many of the psalms by heart. Agnes and I read the Bible together, but we need a teacher. I wish we could attend conventicles."

Lady Stewart shook her head. "It's a crime to do that. The king sends his dragoons to fall upon them." A veil of sadness settled over her face. "It's difficult to forgive their savage attacks on innocent people gathered for worship." She swallowed and then added in a voice so soft that Margaret had to strain to hear her, "It's hard to be living in these killing times."

Killing times! Margaret's stomach began to churn like buttermilk in the making. Did she really want to leave her family and run away to the hills? Was she smart enough to elude the dragoons? If they caught her—she shuddered at the horror—she could be raped. What if they tortured Agnes? Or Mother?

Lady Stewart laid a gentle hand on her shoulder. "Don't be afraid, Margaret. Since God is for us, we need not fear those who are against us."

Lady Stewart's encouraging words were like bread to Margaret's hungry soul. By God's grace, she would remain faithful. She nudged her sister as a little mouse ran over the stone floor to the warmth of the fireplace. *I'll be as helpless as he is once I leave home,* Margaret thought. *But he'll be warm when I am not.* Her stomach tightened as she considered what lay ahead. Thomas and Agnes often did exactly what she did. Father questioned them when he disagreed with their decisions. But he didn't make them change their minds. *Still, joining the Covenanters in the hills is a different story.* She was especially concerned that Agnes, frail as she was, would insist on leaving with her.

"May I ask you something else, Lady Stewart?"

"Of course."

"I know my way around the Galloway Hills. I can hide among the braes and find shelter under a moss-hag if I'm pursued." She smiled at the idea of being wiser than the enemy. "But without a fire, it will be cold. What will I do if I become ill?"

"The hill people will help you."

"But it will still be very cold."

"The hill folk don't all live on the moors during the bitterest parts of winter," Lady Stewart said. "Friends hide some of them in their attics or their cellars. Or in abandoned barns and sheds. When the first hailstones rattle across the moors, many of the hill people move to their indoor hidey holes. They'll find a place for you."

"I could take food with me when I leave Glenvernoch. What will I do when it's gone?"

Lady Stewart's eyes clouded as she looked over Margaret's head. "Some days you will go hungry. Rest assured the others will share with you whatever they have, no matter how little that may be."

Margaret again chewed the inside of her cheek. "I believe the Lord is leading me to leave home," she confided. "Mother and Father love me too much to refuse to let me go." Lady Stewart's comments had helped her make up her mind. Now her warm smile encouraged her to follow her convictions.

"It's a high price we must pay for our beliefs," Lady Stewart said.

Margaret looked into her deep, dark eyes. "I love Jesus more than anything else. I am willing to suffer for him."

"Even if you have to die for him?"

14

SECRET INVITATION

Lady Stewart studied the girls for a minute and then spoke softly. "Next Lord's Day, there's going to be a conventicle not far from here."

Margaret's eyes brightened. Would she finally get to attend a large outdoor service?

"Our beloved leader, Reverend James Renwick, will be preaching. Why don't you come—and bring Thomas with you?"

"James Renwick is coming here?" Margaret's heart raced at the thought of hearing him preach.

"Aye, James Renwick! He's coming to Old Risk castle, near Minnigaff. But," she warned them, "you must not tell anyone. Spies infiltrate our meetings and report who has attended."

"How will we find the meeting place?" Margaret asked.

"I'll show you." She picked up a small stick and began to draw in the ashes near the hearth. As she did so, she pointed out the best route to get there from Glenvernoch. "Study this map carefully," she said. When it looked like the girls understood her directions, she erased it. "We don't keep anything in writing. Do you understand?"

"Aye," the girls responded together.

"Hiding out on the moorlands is difficult and dangerous. But if the dragoons continue to hound us, we may all have to flee to the wilds." Her face softened. "I am your friend. You may come to me for help at any time."

"Thank you, Lady Stewart," Margaret said as the girls rose to take their leave.

"I want to pray for you before you go." She placed her hands on their shoulders. "Father in heaven, bless Margaret and Agnes, and Thomas, too. Guide them and protect them from the dragoons. Help them find their way to the conventicle next Lord's Day. Keep their faith strong. May they bring glory to you. Amen."

"Amen," the girls whispered as Lady Stewart wrapped them in a warm embrace.

"Go in peace, my children," she whispered.

The girls patted the terriers, waved goodbye, and headed down the hill and across the familiar path to Glenvernoch. Along the way they talked about the things Lady Stewart had told them. But still they kept alert. One never knew when a dragoon might be lurking about.

Margaret attempted to keep up a conversation with Agnes while wrestling with her concerns for the future. Should she discourage Agnes from attending the conventicle? *She'd be unhappy if she were left behind.* Would Thomas try to stop her from going? She didn't think so. *He has a sharp mind for a fifteen-year-old.* If she escaped to the hills, Agnes would want to go with her. How could a sickly child like her little sister survive during a cold winter? *Please, God,* Margaret prayed silently, *show me what to do. And show Agnes, too.*

It was midafternoon when they arrived home. "How is Lady Stewart?" Mother asked. "Is she well?"

"Aye," Margaret answered. She sensed her mother wanted to know more about their visit, but they were sworn to secrecy. "She treated us kindly."

"She said we could visit her any time," Agnes added.

The girls went outside before Mother could question them further. Margaret had to know if Agnes understood the risks in attending the forbidden field meeting. And she needed to tell Thomas about it. Her stomach twisted into a slipknot at the thought of confronting her father again. Then she thought of Mr. Colquhoun. *What if he has reported my absence?* Dragoons were usually quick to track down people for any offense. *Why should I worry myself sick over something that might happen? But this is only Monday,* she cautioned herself. *Jesus, protect me.* Her breath came in ragged gasps. Agnes looked at her with questioning eyes.

"I'm all right," Margaret said. Then, nodding toward the byre, she added, "Let's find a place to talk." She hoped Agnes couldn't see how worried she was.

When Thomas offered to make the final check of the cattle before retiring, Margaret followed him to the byre. Looking him in the eye, she said, "Next Lord's Day, I'm going to hear a *real* sermon."

"A real sermon? From Mr. Colquhoun?" Thomas laughed. "Impossible!"

Margaret responded with fierce determination. "I am going to a big conventicle."

Thomas's face turned white. "You're doing *what?*"

"There's going to be a conventicle next Sunday near Minnigaff," she answered with quiet awe. "Lady Stewart told us about it. Reverend James Renwick is coming to preach at Old Risk castle." Her voice rose with excitement. "She encouraged Agnes and me to attend. She said we should bring you with us."

Thomas's jaw dropped, and his eyes widened. "Margaret," he said, his voice scarcely more than a whisper, "do not even think of it! We're forbidden to attend secret services." He struggled to regain his composure. "You could have your ears slashed for listening to Reverend Renwick. The dragoons spy out the meetings. They attack them with swords and lances and pikes. They grab the ministers first, but they give no quarter to anyone."

Margaret's heart leaped into her throat. She had wanted to hear Reverend Renwick speak ever since he returned to Scotland. This was the first time she'd known in advance where a conventicle was to be held. She chewed her lip as she weighed the dangers against her desire to meet the young preacher. Her determination overcame her fears. "I want to meet James Renwick," she said with a look that meant nothing could change her mind.

Thomas shook his head. "Claverhouse and Lagg abuse Covenanters, no matter their age—or gender," he said, his voice still unsteady.

"I won't let them chain me with fear, Thomas. Finally I'm going to hear a real minister preach."

She expected another protest from her brother. Instead his furrowed brow relaxed and a twinkle came into his eyes. "I've never been to Old Risk castle," he said. "If it's near Minnigaff, I can find it." He smiled at her. "Do you remember those tasty sparling Fergus and I caught last spring in the River Cree? We were fishing near Minnigaff when we caught them."

Margaret nodded. "Lady Stewart showed us the meeting place on a map," she said.

"Did she give you a copy?"

Margaret shook her head. "She drew it in the ashes on the hearth and then wiped it out. It's too risky to carry a map."

As she spoke of the danger, her thoughts scattered down unpleasant routes. What if the conventicle were attacked and they were caught by the dragoons? Sometimes they stuck lighted matches between women's fingers to force them to tell where their husbands were hiding. They blindfolded children and threatened them by firing muskets over their heads to get them to betray their parents. *Jesus, I'm scared. Please make me bold enough to take the risk.* Shaking off her fears, she looked at Thomas and asked, "Would you like to see the map? I could scratch it out on the ground."

Thomas looked doubtful. She could tell he wasn't sure he could trust her memory. "We've drawn it several times since we got home." She picked up a sturdy stick and began to mark the ground with deliberate movements. "Here's Minnigaff," she said, "and over here is Old Risk castle. Here's the River Cree, and this is Penkiln Burn. We go from here to here to here." She pointed to another spot. "The conventicle will be held in a deep hollow right behind the castle."

Thomas nodded as the studied the map. "We'll find it," he said, as he rubbed the map out with his right boot. "But will Father and Mother let us go to the conventicle?"

"We won't tell them our plans. If they're questioned, they can honestly say they don't know where we are." Margaret squeezed her eyes shut. *Oh, God, it breaks my heart to put them at risk.* She hated having to choose between obeying the Scriptures and obeying her parents.

"We must honor the promises we made to the Lord," Thomas said. "Like you, I intend to keep the covenant—and I'd like to go to the conventicle. But what about Agnes? Can she walk that far?"

"She wants to go, too," Margaret said. "She tires easily, but we can stop to let her rest."

Thomas nodded. "Well, then, how are we going to get away without Mother and Father knowing?"

"We'll set out as soon as they leave for kirk. It will be a long day, so we'll need to take food with us."

"Good thinking," Thomas said as they walked toward the house.

That night when she said her final prayers, Margaret thanked the Lord that they'd be attending the conventicle. *Please, God, don't let anything stop us from getting there.*

15
Disobedient Children

During the rest of the week, Margaret thought of little else but the upcoming conventicle near Old Risk castle. Now that she really was going to attend the secret meeting, she could scarcely contain herself. She and Thomas had worked out their plans to slip off as soon as their parents left for kirk.

While the two of them grew more excited, Agnes remained pensive. Sensing her fears, Margaret tried to reassure her by singing. In a clear, high voice, she sang a few favorite verses from the Psalter:

> God is our refuge and our strength,
> in straits a present aid;
> Therefore, although the earth remove,
> we will not be afraid.

Margaret remained wary but happy that she would soon meet James Renwick. Her absence from kirk the previous Sunday meant the dragoons could come banging on the door at any moment. She prayed for safety as she left the farmhouse to milk the cows. Sitting on the milking stool, she chewed her lower lip, dreading the confrontation they would face on Sunday morning.

What will Father do when Thomas and Agnes refuse to go to kirk? Sighing, she moved on to the next cow. Father hadn't forced her to attend last week, but Thomas and Agnes were younger, and Agnes was timid. Would she change her mind if pressured? *I want them to go to the conventicle with me, but only if they understand the risks.* She wished she could talk with Fergus about the situation. Her eyes misted, and she wiped them with the back of her hand. Perhaps he'd already fled to Drumjargon.

On Saturday she and Agnes helped to prepare extra food for the Lord's Day. Agnes set the bannocks on the shelf while Margaret went to the larder with the boiled beef Mother had prepared as a special treat.

That evening, after the supper trappings had been cleared away, Father read a brief passage of Scripture and led them in prayer. As he closed the Bible, Thomas spoke to him. "Father, I have something to say."

"Speak."

Thomas swallowed and then began. "I'm not going to kirk tomorrow."

Margaret winced at her mother's cry and watched her twist the folds in her skirt. Turning to Father, she saw his face cloud as though he had been butted in the stomach by a ram. The muscles of his jaw tightened, and a strange sound erupted from his throat. He flung his hands flat on the table, rattling the tin candlestick. Learning across it, he stared into Thomas's eyes. "You what?"

Thomas leveled a look at him and repeated his statement. "I am not going to kirk tomorrow."

Father drew back and balled his hands into fists. He shot an accusing glance at Margaret and then looked back at Thomas. His lips moved, but no words came out. Silence as heavy as the heaviest mist on the moors filled the room.

Margaret studied her father's hands. They were large and calloused, roughened by years of hard work that had made him a prosperous heritor. He was proud of his holdings and proud that one day his land lease would be passed down to Thomas. By staying away from kirk, they were putting all he had worked for in jeopardy. *I wish these things were not so, but we must do what is right in the eyes of the Lord*, she reminded herself lest she weaken out of concern for her earthly father.

In time Father regained his composure enough to speak. Again searching Thomas's eyes as if to find a way to make him change his mind, he asked, "Why?"

"Because I own the covenant," Thomas said. "Jesus is the head of the kirk, not King Charles. God does not have first place in the heart of the king or in Mr. Colquhoun. My conscience will not let me return."

"I own the covenant, too," Father said. "I merely give the appearance of complying to save what I've worked for all these years."

Margaret's stomach convulsed into a tighter knot. She knew her father loved the Lord, and he loved his Galloway cattle. She wished he didn't have to dishonor one to save the other.

"Father," Thomas said, with a greater maturity than Margaret had ever heard in his voice, "if I were in your place, I might feel the same." He looked at him without blinking. "But

King Jesus is head of our kirk, and you have taught us to obey him. I refuse to pretend to be loyal to King Charles."

Their father's shoulders sagged. He turned to Agnes and said, "So be it. Mother and Agnes will go with me tomorrow."

"No, Father," Agnes said. "I'm not going either."

Mother winced, her face pale as ash. Father stared at the three of them as though they were strangers. "May God forgive me if I am in error. I am doing what I can to protect all of you." He limped out of the room, a defeated man.

Mother rose to follow, but he closed the door before she reached it. Returning to her chair beside the hearth, she lowered her head in her hands and sobbed. Margaret and Agnes knelt beside her, each taking one of her hands into their own. By and by she raised her head. Margaret saw love in her red-rimmed eyes. Her lips remained pressed together tightly as if she did not trust her voice.

Not knowing what else to do, Margaret and Agnes picked up the bonnets they were knitting for Father and Thomas. Mother had spent many hours spinning the blue-gray wool from Father's sheep. A few more hours of knitting and the bonnets would be done. Now and then Margaret felt Mother's eyes upon them, but she said nothing.

When it was time for bed, the girls put their knitting aside. "Good night, Mother," Agnes said, gave her a hug, and then climbed the ladder to her bed.

Margaret embraced her mother. "We love you, Mother," she whispered, "but we can't break our covenant vow."

This time Mother looked into her eyes. "I understand that, Margaret." Mother's eyes filled with tears. "But I am afraid of what will happen to you."

Margaret could not discount her mother's fears. She wanted to comfort her, but how could she do that when she was so frightened she could scarcely keep her teeth from chattering? She hugged her, whispered good night, and prayed her trembling legs would carry her safely up the ladder.

16

CONVENTICLE AT OLD RISK CASTLE

Margaret did not sleep well. Her eyes popped open long before time to arise. Agnes had spent much of the night tossing about in the bed they shared. *Today I am going to hear James Renwick preach.* Each time Margaret thought of that, a thrill swooped through her. Before she crept out of the warm nest where she, too, had thrashed about for hours, she asked the Lord to help their parents understand why they had to go to the forbidden meeting . . . or at least accept their children's decision. Joy bubbled up in her heart. *Thank you for bringing James Renwick to us.*

She pulled last year's woolen dress over her shift and climbed down the ladder. As she headed out to milk the cows, she was glad she didn't have to talk with Mother and Father. It would have been difficult to hide her joy.

When she returned with the milk, Mother was setting yesterday's oatcakes on the table. The family ate in silence. Several times during the meal, Margaret felt her mother's gaze on her. But when she looked into her eyes, she could read nothing. After breakfast, while the girls were helping to clear the table, Mother turned to Margaret and opened her mouth as if to speak. Then, turning abruptly, she followed Father into the adjoining room to prepare for kirk.

The sisters climbed the ladder to the loft, waiting for them to leave. When the heavy outside door closed, they crept downstairs.

Margaret sped to the larder and grabbed the beef she had hidden the night before. Agnes wrapped six oatcakes in a cloth while Thomas filled a skin with buttermilk. They could drink from the burns, but the milk would taste good, too. They didn't know how long it would take to get to their destination. Or how difficult the trip might be. And they had no idea how long the conventicle would last. Margaret and Agnes gathered up the food parcels, and Thomas picked up the buttermilk.

"Thank you, Jesus, that we're going to hear your word today," Margaret whispered.

"Protect us, Lord. Help us find our way to Old Risk castle," Thomas prayed. "Don't let us get separated or lost."

"Please, Jesus, help me not to be afraid," Agnes murmured.

Margaret wrapped her arms around her sister. Thomas took one last look around. "Let's go," he said.

The girls followed him down the path behind the byre. It would lead them to their first landmark, a tall cairn located about three miles from Glenvernoch. They hastened over the moors and through the hills in silence, not stopping until they reached the cairn. After a refreshing drink from a nearby burn, they hurried on.

About an hour later, Margaret spotted the second cairn on a distant hill. When they reached it, they rested again. "Our next landmark is the River Cree," she said to encourage Agnes. "We follow it until we find a place to ford it. Then we'll be in Minnigaff. From there we'll find an old trail that leads up a hill to Old Risk castle."

Margaret's anticipation grew when they crossed the Cree. To avoid being questioned, the three crept through the fringes of the village. As they eased their way along in single file, Margaret heard footsteps. "Shhh!" she whispered.

Thomas glanced about. "Pull your shawls over your heads, and stay close to me." Entire families dressed in their best apparel came into view. Their steps were purposeful and their conversation quiet. The Wilsons fell in behind them, confident that they were also on their way to Old Risk castle. The numbers grew as others appeared from out of the surrounding hills and moved along as silent as the morning mist.

Thomas and his sisters followed the crowd up the west side of Larg Valley. Like a gently flowing stream, hundreds of people made their way toward the old castle. It stood like a stone sentinel at the top of a hill. In a sheltered hollow behind it lay a deep valley wide enough to hold a large congregation. The wind whistling through the surrounding hills would scatter the sound of singing and Reverend Renwick's voice.

The people picked their way down into the hidden valley and seated themselves on the ground in an orderly manner. Margaret, Thomas, and Agnes followed in their wake. More and more families surrounded them until there was scarcely room to move. A family carrying their wee bairn sat down beside Margaret. An air of anticipation wafted over the congregation as the people waited for the conventicle to begin.

Margaret looked around at the hundreds of believers gathered for the service. She had no idea there were so many who faithfully owned the covenant. At some distance across from where they sat, she spotted Laird and Lady Stewart and her maid. Her gaze next settled on the four lookouts stationed up on the hill, alert and ready to sound a warning. Their presence gave her comfort, but their muskets were a grim reminder that it was dangerous to be here. She had waited so long for this day. If the service didn't begin soon, her heart would burst with anticipation.

A hush fell across the congregation as someone sur-rounded by a half dozen armed young Covenanters threaded his way through their midst. He approached the makeshift pulpit with energetic steps and raised his hand in greeting. Surely this slender young man wasn't Reverend Renwick. Why, he didn't look any older than Fergus! But, if it wasn't James Renwick, who could it be?

17

DRAGOONS!

Margaret stared at the bonny young man who had just mounted the huge stone that would serve as his pulpit. She wasn't expecting John the Baptizer, but this man didn't meet her expectations either. He was small in stature. Almost frail. Blue eyes. Fair hair. Pale complexion. Could he be the revered minister who had been stirring the Covenanters to action wherever he went? When he pronounced a blessing on the gathering in a mellow, comforting voice, she knew it was indeed Reverend Renwick. One of the men announced the forty-sixth psalm and began to sing the first lines.

> God is our refuge and our strength,
> In straits a present aid;
> Therefore, although the earth remove,
> we will not be afraid.

Margaret's heart leaped with joy that her favorite verses were chosen. She joined the others, singing softly. Gradually their voices rose with the assurance that God was watching over them. He would be their refuge through stormier days ahead. After the psalm, the congregation joined in prayer, thanking God for allowing them to come to Old Risk, where they felt safe to worship together. They prayed for the one who was about to share the Scriptures with them and baptize their bairns. They asked for protection when they made their way home after the conventicle.

As the soft notes of the psalm faded away, Reverend Renwick stepped up to the pulpit and began to read from the book of Revelation. His clear, calm voice resonated across the hollow.

Fear none of those things which thou shalt suffer: behold, the devil shall cast some of you into prison, that ye may be tried; and ye shall have tribulation ten days: be thou faithful unto death, and I will give thee a crown of life.

He paused, contemplating the Covenanters seated on the ground below him. By coming to this meeting, they had risked their lives, but so had he. Margaret studied his face. Anyone who led the dragoons to him would be rewarded. Yet he appeared completely at peace. Reverend Renwick gazed up at the lookouts surrounding them on the hill above. Then turning his face to the spiritually hungry congregation before him, he presented a simple message of God's love for his people.

Margaret listened with breathless attention for the next couple of hours as Reverend Renwick explained the Scriptures. Jesus loved them so much he died for their sins. Troubles lay ahead of them, and the minister urged them to cling to God. "He will be with you through the difficulties that he allows to come into your life," he said. "He is your refuge and strength. When you walk through darkness, he will light your pathway. Cling to him. He is with you even when you cannot see him."

Though surrounded by hundreds of Covenanters, Margaret felt the message was spoken directly to her, wrapping her in the Lord's presence. For years she had yearned to hear him speak directly to her. Now she sensed his closeness as never before. She listened with rapt attention, never taking her face off the minister. She had no idea when she might hear another sermon. She wanted to absorb every word so that she would never forget it. *I will be faithful, Jesus,* she promised in her heart, *even if I must die for you.*

As she listened, she felt something like raindrops on her cheeks. Surprised, she looked up at the sky. It was not raining. She wiped her tears with the hem of her skirt. God loved her with an everlasting love, and she would rest in that assurance.

Margaret sat enraptured as James Renwick ended his message and invited parents with bairns to be baptized to bring them forward. As they began to do so, he raised his eyes once again toward the lookouts. "By God's grace, we have worshiped together in peace," he said. "We will close our service with the thirty-first Psalm."

Margaret lifted her voice with the others, and their exuberant praises echoed across the broad hollow. Before they had finished their song, four musket shots whistled through the air, each one echoing its warning.

"Dragoons!" someone screamed.

Glancing upward, Margaret saw the lookouts slumped to the ground. At that moment a dragoon cleared the brow of the hill.

"God is still with us!" Reverend Renwick shouted above the din of the frightened worshipers. "Run for your lives!"

Immediately armed young men swarmed around him and whisked him out of sight and into the safety of the surrounding hills. People on the fringes bolted out of the way of those sitting on the ground in front of them. Fathers snatched up young children. Mothers clutched their bairns to their breasts.

Thomas grabbed Agnes's hand. "We must stay together," he said dragging her toward the tangled heather on the edge of the hollow. "God will help us."

Margaret reached for Aggie's other hand, but the fleeing worshipers swept her along, separating her from Thomas and Agnes. She cringed as the screams of the fallen echoed around her. Would the slaughter never stop?

Terror clutched at her throat as she fled deeper into the hills. She must find her family. As she stumbled along through the tangled heather, she remembered she had to climb the hill to get to the castle. From there she'd be able to see the landmarks she needed to guide her home.

Keeping her eyes focused on the old castle, she scrambled up some scree and picked her way toward the top of the hill. Fear of being overtaken by darkness spurred her to climb faster. With pounding heart and aching legs, she scurried upward. When she reached the top, she paused to catch her breath. Now she could see the path leading down to Minnigaff. She chewed her lower lip and pictured her sister's blue eyes clouding up as she tried to be brave. *Aggie will be frightened and tired, so they will travel slowly*, she reasoned. If she hurried, she should be able to catch up with them. She quickened her pace with longer strides. *Please, God, help me find them.*

Relieved to be on familiar ground, her mind returned to the conventicle. Her joy at hearing James Renwick preach had been marred by the attack from the dragoons, but she knew her heart had been changed. She put her hands over her ears to erase the screams that seemed lodged in them. She prayed for the wounded and for the families of the fallen. And then she prayed for James Renwick. Awed by the new awareness of God's presence in her life, she hoped she'd hear him speak again.

She skirted Minnigaff and crept around the trees in silence. The conventicle had strengthened her desire to follow Jesus wherever he led, no matter the cost. She reviewed the day's events as she crossed the River Cree and retraced her morning steps along the river toward the fourth landmark.

As the cairn came into sight, she saw Thomas and Agnes resting against it. She brushed away her tears with the back of her hand and hastened toward them. When she reached them, she nearly crushed them with her hugs.

Relieved to be together again, the three resumed their journey home. At first they walked in silence, their voices frozen by what they had experienced. Eventually they were able to talk about the attack. The Lord had spared them and they were grateful, but Margaret worried about what Agnes might be thinking and feeling.

As if reading her mind, Agnes said, "I'm never going to turn away from Jesus." When Margaret smiled at her, she continued. "Nobody is going to make me disown the covenant!"

"Nor me!" Thomas said. He looked at the surrounding moorland. "We need to hurry on lest the gloaming overtake us."

Margaret could see in Thomas's bright eyes that he had renewed his commitment to Jesus. She was glad he was shepherding them back to Glenvernoch. The Lord had enabled them to worship at the conventicle and had delivered them from the dragoons. Her joy seemed complete ... until she considered what would happen when they arrived home.

18

SAFELY HOME

It was nearly dark when the weary young people reached Glenvernoch. They were scarcely within sight of their home when Mother burst out of the house. The alarm in her eyes and on her drawn face showed them how frightened she had been over their long absence. Agnes fell into her mother's arms and dissolved into tears. Mrs. Wilson looked at Thomas and Margaret and in a choked voice said, "I'm glad you're home."

Father appeared at the door, and his body moved forward woodenly. He studied each of his children's faces as if they were strangers. When he spoke, his eyes had a faraway look and his voice seemed to come from another world. "Today you have disappointed me," he said, "but I am relieved you have returned." He drew in a long breath and let it out slowly. "Come inside. We'll talk later." He turned and plodded into the farmhouse.

Mother hastened to the larder and returned with beef and a pitcher of milk. She set them on the table and went to the shelf for the oatcakes. "Eat, my children," she urged. Margaret looked questioningly at her parents. In answer to Margaret's unspoken question, her mother said, "Your father and I are not hungry." Anxious about the impending talk with Father, Margaret ate in uneasy silence.

As they finished their meal, Agnes fought to keep her eyes open. Mother put an arm around her and led her to the ladder. She stood at the foot while Agnes climbed to her loft bed. Meanwhile, Father maintained a stony silence. Thomas shrugged his shoulders as he exchanged glances with Margaret.

Finally Father rose like an arthritic old man and planted his hands on the table. His chin trembled as he spoke. "Mr. Colquhoun did not call the roll this morning." Sighing as though a heavy weight had been lifted from his shoulders, he went on. "But that doesn't mean he didn't notice your absence. Sooner or later he'll report you as disorderly," he warned, "and then our whole family will suffer." He brushed his hand across his wrinkled forehead and looked straight at Margaret, his piercing eyes willing her to change her mind. "You can protect us all by returning to kirk," he croaked.

Margaret felt like she'd swallowed a bannock whole. Now it was lodged in her throat, and her words couldn't find a path around it. She longed for those Sunday evenings when her father took the Bible from the shelf and read to them. Back then he was enthusiastic about what he was reading. Now he read a few verses aloud, but his interest in the Scriptures had diminished as the number of dragoons in the area increased. *He's not being taught, so he has nothing new to teach us*, she said to herself.

Turning to her father, she blinked back her tears and said, "We love you and Mother. I'm sorry we've disappointed you." She swallowed and then went on. "Mr. Renwick warned us that we must suffer for our faith. But Jesus will be with us through our trials." She paused as if seeing a vision. "If need be, he will give us strength to die for him."

Mother, seated again at the table, gasped and twisted the hem of her apron.

"Father," Thomas said, speaking with great respect, "we have vowed to remain faithful to Jesus no matter the cost."

Silence as deep as the gathering shadows of night settled over the family. The Wilsons had taught their children to be strong-willed, to do what they felt was right. But they would pay dearly for their disobedience to the king's rules, as would the entire family. Pain spread over Gilbert Wilson's face as though he had an abscessed tooth. He looked long into the solemn eyes of his children and left the room.

Margaret awakened the next morning, determined to talk with her mother about the conventicle. Today was laundry day, so they would have time together while they worked. Carrying the water, heating it over the fire, and then scrubbing the clothing would keep them busy for hours. After breakfast, the girls grabbed their buckets and headed to the spring. If the three of them worked diligently, they'd be finished by noon.

After the water heated and the clothes soaked a bit, Margaret picked up her father's linen shirt and began to scrub fiercely. "Mother, why doesn't the Lord answer our prayers and end this struggle with His Royal Highness?"

Mother swished a shift in the soapy water as she answered. "The king insists he is head of the kirk by divine right." She grimaced. "That's why he passed that dreadful Test Act three years ago. The only thing we can do is ask the Lord to protect us until he deals with King Charles."

Margaret scrubbed her father's shirt as though it were the enemy. "I'm glad our family has not been ordered to swear the Test."

Mother dropped the shift into the wash water and turned her troubled eyes to Margaret. "So am I," she said, "but I fear the day is coming when we will have to do that." She picked up the shift and continued. "I'm pleased that your heart is surrendered to Jesus. I love him, too, but . . ." She lowered her voice and whispered softly, "My faith is not as strong as yours. Your father and I will do what we must to protect you children and our property."

"I wish we didn't have to choose between obeying the Lord and obeying His Royal Highness."

Mother sighed as though all the hills of Galloway were settling on her shoulders. "I wish the same thing," she whispered. Her chin quivered as she tried to speak. Finally the words tumbled out. "Laurie of Maxwelton showed up at kirk yesterday!" She turned back to the laundry and scrubbed until her knuckles began to bleed.

"Laurie!" Agnes shrieked.

Margaret grabbed her sister's hand. "That Judas!" she muttered under her breath. "The cowardly beast skulks about spying on people so he can report them in exchange for a few coins." His presence at kirk meant trouble for her. Big trouble!

She had no doubts but that Laurie of Maxwelton would report her. But he was devious and greedy—and patient when it was to his benefit. He would wait until he could curry the greatest favor from Lagg or Graham of Claverhouse before he made his report. If only she know when that would be.

I must leave home, Margaret thought. *But I cannot run away until I sense a clear direction from the Lord that the time is right.* Meanwhile she would return to kirk with the rest of the family. That would give her time to work out details for her escape.

During the next few months, the Wilsons heard reports that more Covenanters were being killed for refusing to take the Test. Consequently, James Renwick suggested that they carry arms. In mid-November Father and Thomas went to Minnigaff to get some harnesses. They found the village in an uproar.

"James Renwick has posted a declaration on the Mercat Cross," Father said when they arrived back home. Margaret glanced at Thomas to see if that was good or bad news. Father answered her unspoken question. "Mr. Renwick has vowed that Covenanters will defend their faith with arms, if need be."

"That's treason!" declared Mr. Colquhoun at kirk, echoing the King's Privy Council. A few weeks later he read to his congregation the council's response to the Renwick Declaration, the Abjuration Oath. "Everyone must renounce James Renwick and his declaration and declare their allegiance to King Charles," Mr. Colquhoun said.

At first the king's forces acted only against the extremists, led by Renwick himself. But before long all Covenanters were at risk. This insidious action turned southwestern Scotland into a war zone. Killing became more frequent as the troopers acted with greater violence. Savage persecutions were commonplace, and Covenanters' blood flowed more freely than before. For the Covenanters, this pernicious oath was the last straw! Many of them chose life with Jesus rather than compromise their faith.

I will flee to the hills before I swear such an oath, Margaret said to herself.

19
WARNING!

Several months passed with no tattling on the part of Laurie of Maxwelton. Margaret forgot her worries about him as she grieved over Fergus's absence and the deaths of hundreds of Covenanters who would not take an oath they didn't believe. Bloodthirsty soldiers sent by the king began to force everyone into submission. The time had come to escape.

Agnes and Thomas were determined to go with her. They planned to leave the following Lord's Day after Father led them in evening devotions. They would slip off to the moss-hag that Thomas had selected for their hideaway, the place where he and Fergus met after John and Robert fled to Ireland.

As the family was finishing breakfast on Saturday, Margaret swallowed, took a deep breath, and said, "Father, we've decided to—" A loud, persistent knocking drowned out her voice. A knocking that signified trouble.

Dragoons! Margaret froze, her mouth still open. *Dear God, protect us.*

A cry of alarm escaped Mother's lips as she and Father exchanged anxious glances. Father motioned for her to stay behind as he hastened to the door and opened it.

Fergus Walker pushed his way past him and into the farmhouse. Relief and then anger spread over Father's face. Fergus was so agitated he could scarcely speak. "I've come to warn you that—" he panted and glanced into Margaret's pale face "—you've been reported! For not attending kirk."

"That cannot be!" said Father. "Not one of us has been absent the past few months."

"It is true!" Fergus said, with an intensity that could not be doubted.

Father groaned. "God help us." He fixed his eyes on Fergus. "How do you know that Margaret was reported? I thought you left this area long ago."

Fergus stammered. "I did leave. Four months ago. But yesterday I planned to steal home undercover to see my father and mother. I sneaked into Wigtown in the gathering dusk—to buy some ribbons for Margaret." He looked at her with anxious eyes. "As I passed by the tolbooth, I heard angry voices. I recognized Lagg's." He looked at Margaret while he caught his breath. "He's sending the dragoons after you." He blinked and added, "I hid in the shadows while I eavesdropped. I saw Laurie of Maxwelton swagger out." Fergus's voice dropped to a bitter whisper. "He was counting the coins in his hand!"

"That good-for-naught wretch!" Father muttered.

Mother gasped. Her hand flew to her forehead. She collapsed on the hearth and began to sob. "My bairns. My bairns. Robert and John are gone. I cannot bear to lose the others."

Margaret squared her shoulders and took a deep breath. *A pox on Laurie of Maxwelton. And on Grierson of Lagg!* She shot a glance at Thomas. "Tonight!" she mouthed to him. Thomas nodded.

In the hubbub that followed, Fergus was forgotten. Father put an arm around Mother and bowed his head. His lips moved but there was no sound. He finished his prayer and then looked into Margaret's eyes. "I was afraid this would happen."

He turned to Thomas and Agnes. "I begged you not to stay home from kirk that Lord's Day. I should have insisted that you attend." He dropped to the bench and covered his face while Mother wiped her tears with her apron.

Margaret's attention was fixed on Fergus. *He has risked his life to come warn us.* The depth of his love filled her with warmth. *I wish I could have run away with him. I hope he understands why I couldn't.* His warning meant they must change their plans. *Grierson can have Thomas hanged, and who knows what he might do to Agnes and me? Well, he'll have to find us first.*

She prayed he never would—and that they'd be strong enough and brave enough to survive away from home. She hated having to slink away like a thief in the night. She'd already given up Fergus. She'd miss her parents—and Mother's hot mutton broth and fresh oatcakes—and her barley bannocks and pease porridge. Would she ever again feel her warm hugs or hear her comforting prayers around the glowing hearth?

"Father," Margaret said, "I own the covenant. To break my oath would make me as sinful as His Royal Highness for breaking the covenant he swore at his coronation. I cannot do that." She stared into the darkening corners of the room as she thought about the future. If only her faith did not demand so much. "If we stay here, I will be forced to swear something I do not believe. You know I cannot do that."

Father raised his head. His eyes were glazed, and his lower lip trembled.

"Agnes and I are going with Margaret," Thomas said. "The Lord will help us through whatever lies ahead."

Tears coursed down their faces as Janet and Gilbert Wilson gathered their children into their arms. They knelt together to pray. Father tried to find his voice. "M-M-Merciful Father, we commit our children to you. Please watch over them." His voice faltered. "Help them find food and shelter. Blind the eyes of the dragoons so they can't find them and . . . and . . . and may we all be together with you one day in heaven."

Mother wiped her eyes and hurried to the larder to gather provisions for her children.

The tumult having subsided, Fergus turned to Mr. Wilson. "May I speak a word with Margaret?"

Father nodded, and the two stepped outside. Fergus pulled Margaret into his arms and held her close to his racing heart. When he was able to speak he whispered, "I'll be praying for you every day." He drew back, holding her at arm's length, and asked, "Will you think of me, Margaret?"

"Aye," she said, unable to utter another word, fearing she would never see him again.

Fergus traced the features of her face as though etching them into his mind. His warm lips brushed hers. "Goodbye, Margaret. May God keep you safe," he murmured. "Now I must go."

"God keep you safe, Fergus," she whispered. She stood rooted in the doorway until the man she loved disappeared from view. When she could no longer see him, she went inside.

The family spent the rest of the day preparing for the escape. That evening, while Mother stuffed a large basket with bannocks, oatcakes, and leftover beef, Margaret and

Agnes climbed the ladder to the loft. After pulling on as much of their clothing as they could wear, they rolled extra stockings into their blankets. Margaret tucked the whistle Fergus had made for her into a safe place in the center of her bedroll.

When the girls descended the ladder with their cumbersome bundles, Thomas's bedroll lay on the floor near the door. He was kneeling beside the hearth tying together some sticks of peat to burn the first night.

Had there been a full moon, they would have needed no light to find their way to the moss-hag where they would stay until they found the hill people. But the night was dark. Father sat near Thomas, cobbling together a torch light from broken peats and whatever else he could find. When he finished, he handed it to Thomas and disappeared into the next room. He returned with his best knife. "Take it, son," he said. "You will need it more than I will."

"Father will leave food for you near the big flat rock at the head of Boughty Burn," Mother said.

The young people gathered about the hearth with Mother and Father to pray for the Lord's protection. Amid their tears they professed their love for the Lord and for their parents. Mother and Father kissed them good-bye and went to their sleeping quarters exhausted with grief.

Late that evening, when the sliver of moon disappeared behind the clouds, Thomas lighted the torch from the glowing fireplace embers. The three wrapped themselves in their warmest woolen cloaks and stepped out into the night. Agnes sighed softly as the door closed behind them. Margaret looked back in a last farewell to Mother and Father—and to the home she loved. *God, help us survive in the dangerous, boggy moorland.*

Guided by Father's torch, they picked their way through the darkness toward their hiding place. As they walked, Margaret's heart pounded in her ears. Thomas and Agnes looked to her for direction. Was it her strong faith that was leading them away from their grieving parents? Or was it her arrogance? She wasn't sure. And she had no idea what lay ahead.

20

LIVING UNDER
A MOSS-HAG

Thomas tucked his bedroll under his left arm along with the peat sticks. Holding his torch high, he led his sisters on a roundabout route to their destination. Agnes, clutching her bedroll to her chest, followed closely behind. Margaret held her bedroll under one arm and Mother's food basket in the other. She chuckled at the plump silhouettes in front of her as they plodded along in the shadowy light. "We look like giant sausages with legs," she whispered loud enough for the others to hear.

When they stopped for a short rest Margaret said, "We can sing softly under our breath, or in our heads. That will make the time go faster."

Content to let Thomas take the lead, Margaret followed her own advice and sang her favorite psalms as they trudged along. When they reached the moss-hag, Thomas helped the girls slip beneath the cut in the hillside, now overhung with moss and heather. They dropped their bedrolls onto the ground and collapsed on top of them. Thomas looked about for a solid place to set his torch, which had burned itself down considerably.

"We'll light a peat before the torch burns completely out," he said. Margaret sensed he was concerned about Agnes. So was she. Would she be terrorized by the darkness?

Agnes surprised her with her pluck. "You don't have to do that for me," she said.

"You are a brave little sister." Margaret edged close to her and wrapped her in her arms. "But I'd like it better with a wee bit of light until we go to sleep." She untied her bedroll. "Let's put my blanket on the ground. We can roll up close together in yours, Aggie, and pull mine around us." As she spoke, she couldn't help giggling at the thought of two fat sausages stuffed into a blanket.

Thomas laid the slimmest peat against the dying torch. When it began to smolder, he placed the other sticks across it. If he did this correctly, they'd be able to rekindle a blaze in the morning. Clumps of peat could be found anywhere, so they could gather more the next day. He curled up inside his blanket and rolled over against Agnes. With Margaret on one side and him on the other, she should be snug inside her blanket. "Good night, girls," he said.

"Good night, Thomas," Margaret replied. Agnes was already asleep. And before Father's torchlight burned itself out, so were Thomas and Margaret. Lying close to each other in such confined quarters, they generated enough body heat to keep warm until dawn.

When they awakened the next morning, they talked about what to do first. "We need to make this place warmer," Thomas said. He glanced up to where shafts of light were slicing into the darkness of their hiding place. "There's plenty of heather around to cover the top. That will keep the cold out and our body warmth in."

Margaret unrolled herself from the blankets and sat up. "First, let's eat something." She reached out for the food basket and set it on the blanket between herself and Agnes. Before they ate, Thomas led them in prayer. "Thank you, Lord, for bringing us to the moss-hag and for the food Mother packed for us."

Feeling uncertain about when and how they'd find more food once the basket was empty, Margaret pulled out the beef and tore one slice into three pieces. She handed Thomas and Agnes each a bannock and took one out for herself. Mother had included a skin of buttermilk. In the dim light she had to feel around to tell what else was in the basket. In the bottom she found three tin cups and their horn spoons. *God bless Mother.* She poured each some buttermilk. They ate their breakfast with little conversation.

"We're safe when we're under the moss-hag," Thomas said when they were finished, "but we must never let down our guard." He paused as if he were rethinking his plans for the morning. "Margaret and I can gather stones to put around our shelter to fill in the gaps. And Agnes, we need you to gather up as many small peats as you can find." With an anxious look, he added, "But above all, we need to keep watch all the time we're outside the moss-hag."

Once the walls were solid, the three of them covered the top with layers of heather. As they worked, Margaret thought about the events of the preceding night. She had been so surprised to see Fergus. *May the Lord bless him for warning us.* By now the dragoons were probably pounding on the farmhouse door in Glenvernoch. They would be furious when they didn't find them. Mother would be terrified, and Father would feel helpless against their ruthless behavior. Shivering, she said, "Thomas, we'd better go inside."

Thomas nodded and followed her and Agnes into the shelter. "Since we have to stay hidden, we might as well sleep," Thomas said. "At dusk I will venture out to look for signs of the hill people." He stirred up their little peat fire. Then the trio rolled up in their blankets and slept until late afternoon.

When they awakened, Margaret again portioned out their food. As soon as Thomas felt safe in the gathering darkness, he crept out to explore his surroundings. He and his brothers had combed this territory together in their younger years, but never after sundown. "Be careful, Thomas," Margaret cautioned.

"I will," he promised.

Margaret and Agnes prayed for his protection and that he would find the hill people—or at least some clue that they were nearby. Margaret tried to remember everything Lady Stewart had told them about living in the hills. She worried about Thomas wandering the moors after dark, but she kept her fears to herself. Time crept by ever so slowly as they waited for his return. Eventually he returned—nothing to report. They wrapped themselves in their blankets, rolled as close together as they could get, and slept.

When the girls awakened, Thomas's blanket was empty. "He's just gone outside to relieve himself," Margaret assured Agnes.

Before long Thomas returned with a smile. "Look what I found!" In his right hand he held a large basket. "God is good to us," he said, handing it to Margaret.

"Aye," the girls replied in a reverential whisper.

Margaret stared at the basket. "Lady Stewart told us the Lord would take care of us until we found the hill folk." She handed the basket to Agnes. "Why don't you see what he has sent to us this morning?"

Agnes clutched the precious basket in her hands and slowly removed the cloth covering it. Her eyes widened as she pulled out bannocks, barley cakes, and three thick slices of boiled beef. As she returned the food to the basket, she discovered something in the bottom. She reached in and pulled out a letter. Written on the outside in large print, it said, TO MARGARET.

Margaret's hands trembled as she unfolded the letter and scanned its contents. Tears rolled down her cheeks as she read it first to herself and then aloud:

Dear Margaret,

I have not stopped praying for you since the moment I overheard Lagg's threat. Dragoons are crawling all over Glenvernoch and the surrounding area. They will not give up until they find you. I dare not show my face. I must return to Drumjargon as soon as it appears safe to do so. I have copied some Scriptures to encourage you and Thomas and Agnes.

Mother sends her love and her prayers. I will try to bring you another basket before I leave. God keep you.

Fergus

Tucked inside the letter was a page covered with tiny writing. Margaret held it close to her eyes. Tears of gratitude slid down her cheeks. "It's the book of First John," she whispered when she stopped crying enough to make out the words. She held it to her lips and then tucked it into her pocket. Smiling through her tears she said, "We'll have a bigger breakfast this morning." She picked up the basket as though it were a sacred object and handed it to Thomas. It wasn't manna and quail, but she was as grateful as the hungry children of Israel when God provided food for them.

But what would they do when the basket was empty?

21

ALONE AND WORRIED

After hiding under the moss-hag for five days, Margaret began to worry about food. Father had promised to leave a basket at the head of Boughty Burn, but they hadn't found it. Fergus intended to leave another one before returning to Drumjargon. What if he couldn't? What if they were left with nothing to eat? What if they couldn't find the hill people? And most frightening, what if the dragoons spied them when they were out looking for food? *God help us.*

Two mornings later, she climbed out of the moss-hag with Thomas so he could show her where he'd found the basket that Fergus had left for them. To her delight, she discovered another one. Now they would have food for a few more days. They drank from the burn, but she wished they had something hot to eat or to drink. Some oatcakes fresh from the girdle or a bowl of steaming broth would be most welcome.

At night, the cold earth was their bed and stones were their pillows. Margaret dreamed of home. She longed for a blazing fire to warm her shivering body, but their fire had burned itself out four days ago and they had no way to relight it. She yearned for the comforting smell of bannocks baking on the hearth. Or for a flickering candle to chase away the dismal gloom. But their only light came from the sun by day and the moon and silvery stars at night. She wished they could find the hill folk—and that they didn't have to be constantly on guard for troopers with guns—and dogs.

"Let's all go out tonight to look for the hill people," she said. She prayed again for the Lord to help them.

As they trudged along in the moonlight, Margaret regretted that families were forbidden to have contact with the hill people. Had Grierson and his savage soldiers caught Father stealing out to the moors with a basket of provisions? *Oh, God, please keep Father safe.* Thomas was brave. So was Agnes despite being frail. And she was . . . She couldn't finish the thought. She didn't feel brave, and she didn't feel wise. What she felt was guilt for involving her brother and sister in this harrowing situation.

After several hours of tramping about the frozen moorland, they returned empty-handed to their cold shelter. Huddled together trying to get warm, they discussed their plight. "I could slip home after dark and get food from the larder," Margaret said. "Along the way I might find other hill folk out on the moors for the same reason."

Thomas shook his head. "It's too dangerous."

The idea of sneaking home reminded Margaret of the "brownies." Some people believed these fairy folk came out in the night to do small chores while people were asleep. At times they helped themselves to the bannocks. Some farmers allowed a part of each field to grow high with grass to shelter them. Milkmaids left a bowl of cream for the brownies they believed lived in the byre. Margaret's friend Widow M'Lauchlan explained who the brownies were.

"Brownies are nothing more than persecuted Covenanters," she'd said. "They dare not visit their homes except after dark. They come looking for food."

Now we've become brownies, and we can't risk getting caught, thought Margaret.

The following morning, Margaret awakened before the others. She studied their pinched faces, barely visible beneath the woolen cloaks they had pulled tight around themselves. Agnes shivered in her sleep. *If only we had a bowl of steaming porridge this morning.*

When the others woke up, Margaret suggested they stay wrapped in their blankets and rest until dusk. "Then we'll have more energy to look for food." Thomas agreed. They settled down and were soon fast asleep.

At twilight they left the moss-hag again. They would search every spot once more in hopes of finding food. Once their eyes adjusted to the dark, they quickened their steps to keep warm.

As they crept along, Agnes spotted something near a cairn about a mile from their moss-hag shelter. "Look!" she whispered. "There's something over there. To the right. It wasn't there last night." Running as fast as she dared in the semi-darkness, Margaret came upon a basket wrapped in a piece of worn woolen cloth. When she picked it up, the aroma of fresh baked bannocks wafted out. Her mouth watered, and tears glistened in her eyes. She held the cloth up in the moonlight for the others to see. "It's a piece of Mother's old cloak."

Inside the basket Agnes found six bannocks and six thick oatcakes. "Oh, thank you, Mother, thank you. And thank you,

Jesus." She buried her face in the comforting cloth that smelled of love and home, and she wept.

In her mind's eye Margaret saw her mother mixing meal with milk to make a paste. She watched as she poured it on to the flat girdle hanging over the burning peats. A little batter for oatcakes and more batter for thicker bannocks. She inhaled, remembering the pleasant aroma that filled the farmhouse on baking days. She cast a wistful glance at Thomas and blinked back her tears.

The next day, snowflakes began falling. Thomas frowned as he brushed them from his shoulders. The wind howled across the moors like a wounded animal. "It's covering everything with a powdery sheet," he said as he crept back under the moss-hag.

Margaret pulled her cloak tighter and wished she were home in front of the hearth. "Dear God," she prayed, "we thank you for Mother's tasty bannocks and oatcakes. But we're cold and we're frightened. We don't know where we'll get more food. Please help us find the hill people so we won't be alone." She swallowed so the others wouldn't know she was on the verge of tears. Then she began to sing. "What time I am afraid, I will trust in thee." It was a verse her mother had taught her when she was a little girl. She and Agnes sang it often.

Agnes snuggled close to her. "I w-w-wish we w-w-weren't so c-c-cold," she said.

Margaret wrapped her arms around her sister. "So do I," she whispered through her chattering teeth. Thomas stomped his feet trying to get warm.

Margaret shut her eyes and imagined a blazing pile of peats burning on the hearth. She sniffed, remembering the strong peat reek at home. But there was no magic in their makeshift shelter or in her wishing. She opened her eyes to the brutal reality of life as a runaway.

Thomas moved toward the entrance to their shelter where a little light streamed in. His hands shook as he fumbled through the verses of Scripture they had brought with them until he found the one he wanted. Then he began to read aloud:

My brethren, count it all joy when ye fall into divers temptations. Knowing this, that the trying of your faith worketh patience. But let patience have her perfect work, that ye may be perfect and entire, wanting nothing.

Margaret's shoulders shook. *Wanting nothing? Right now we lack everything!*

"I don't understand that," Agnes said.

"It's from the epistle of James," he told her. "And listen to this. 'If any of you lack wisdom, let him ask of God, that giveth to all men liberally, and upbraideth not; and it shall be given him.'"

Thomas folded the precious Scriptures and put them in a safe place before wrapping his arms around his sisters. "Lord," he prayed, "we're cold. And hungry. And discouraged. We're asking for wisdom and direction. Please lead us to the hill people. For your honor and our good, in Christ's name we pray. Amen."

Margaret gritted her teeth and squared her shoulders. Living on the moors was hard, but she would not compromise her faith and go home. But what if Thomas and Agnes gave up? What then?

22

ANSWERED PRAYERS

That evening, as darkness settled over the moor, Thomas and Margaret split their last bannock and gave half of it to Agnes. Then they ventured out. Their breath froze in front of their faces as they skirted a small snowdrift near their shelter. They must venture farther than they'd gone on previous nights. Since the cold forced them to move about briskly to keep warm, it would be easy to cover more ground. Margaret tried to ignore the hungry lion in her stomach as they hurried along.

They had struggled through the slippery snow for about half a mile when a large cairn loomed before them in the faint moonlight. Thomas hurried toward it. When his sisters caught up with him, he pointed ahead with a wide sweep of his right arm. "Look!" he whispered.

"Where?" Agnes asked, her voice weak and grumpy.

Margaret moved a bit closer and peered over Thomas's shoulder into the darkness. "It looks like a fire!" She stared more intently.

"It *is* a fire! I am going to edge closer to see who's there." He held his finger to his lips and crept forward.

Margaret's heart hammered like hailstones against her chest. Surely that wretched Grierson hadn't sent his dragoons out into the snowy night looking for them. She and Agnes followed at a safe distance as Thomas made his way toward the fire. A few more steps brought him into a clearing where a dozen or so people were kneeling. He was about to step out into the group when an armed man turned and faced him.

Margaret drew back and held her breath until Thomas turned and beckoned to them. Then she grabbed Agnes's hand, and they stumbled forward as fast as they could on cold-numbed feet.

"We've found the hill people," Thomas said.

The trio dropped to their knees to join in their prayers and to feel the warmth of their crackling fire.

"Welcome in the name of our Lord," the leader said when their prayers ended. "Are you hungry?"

Before they could answer, a woman stepped forward. "Please help yourself." She offered them a basket of barley bannocks.

When Agnes responded with a shivery smile, one of the men removed his cloak and wrapped it around her. Another cloak was passed to Margaret and a third to Thomas. While the fugitives ate, the leader said, "We've been watching for you. You are welcome to stay with us. There is safety in numbers." He smiled, and the firelight danced in his eyes. "We will share our food and our shelter." He gestured toward the right. "We live in a cave we've hollowed out, just over that hill. We'll make room for you until the cold forces us to move into the village."

Thomas's face registered relief and gratitude. "Thank you, Mr. . . . Mr. . . ."

"Call me Jonathan."

"We're grateful to you, Jonathan." Thomas paused as if he wanted to ask a question but wasn't sure it was in order. "Is . . . it . . . safe to move into the village?"

"Aye," Jonathan said smiling. "We have friends who hide us each winter. I'm certain they'll find shelter for three more keepers of the covenant." He glanced up at the stars twinkling in the cold, dark sky and added, "We'll be slipping off to those shelters soon." He turned back to Thomas. "Meanwhile you can fish with us in the burns, and we'll teach you to snare wild animals and small birds."

While Thomas went out hunting with the men, the girls warmed themselves by the fire that was kept burning. Being able to wash in warm water brought smiles to their faces.

Three days later Thomas and the men returned to the cave with two large baskets. One was filled with food, and the other contained warm blankets and clothing.

"Where did these things come from?" Margaret asked.

Jonathan smiled. "When it seems safe to venture out, caring people leave baskets where we can find them."

The next morning, when Margaret looked out of the cave, it was snowing hard. Winter had settled in like an unwelcome guest who refused to leave. No one dared venture out in the storm.

As the days went by, the girls helped with the cooking while Thomas fished with the men and hunted for food. Some days they returned with a pigeon or two, or maybe a hare. The women smiled as they prepared the meat and added it to their broth.

When they thought it was safe, several of the men sneaked down to the village under cover of darkness. They knew where to find sympathizers who might spare some bannocks or oatcakes. In gratitude they carefully kept out of sight lest they endanger the friends who shared what they had.

The next five days the men tramped through the snow and cold searching for wild game or baskets left for them. They found nothing. The time had come to move down to warmer quarters.

Through years of persecution, the leaders of the group had searched out abandoned huts built by shepherds, who lived out on the moors with their flock during the summer. They'd become adept at flitting across the moorland like dark shadows. While dragoons might venture onto the fringes in search of them, they wouldn't risk having their horses break their legs by stepping on a moss-hag.

It was necessary for the Covenanters to move out of their cave unnoticed because they were considered outlaws, and many had prices on their heads. Each evening when they gathered to pray, they decided who would leave the next day for their warmer hidey holes. In the morning, those who were chosen went off a few at a time to austere shelters as far away as Carrick and Nithsdale.

Sometimes they hid in attics where homeowners shared their food and blankets. More often their new quarters were deserted farm buildings. There they built fires just large enough to warm their broth or gruel or whatever had been smuggled to them. They left their hiding places only to search for food to fill their empty stomachs or blankets to make their shelters warmer.

Margaret wondered when it would be their turn to leave the cave and where they would go. She soon found out.

"Thomas," Jonathan said several nights later, looking at him and then at his sisters. "Tomorrow I'll take you to a safe place. It will be a long journey."

Margaret was eager to know their destination. "Where are you taking us?"

"I must not tell you or anyone else." Jonathan grimaced. "God forbid that we be stopped by the dragoons. But if we are," his voice dropped to a whisper, "we can't be forced to tell what we don't know." He looked into their puzzled faces. "Trust me," he said. "We will set out immediately after breakfast and our time of prayer."

The next morning it was Margaret's turn to prepare the porridge. As she added the meal to the salted water bubbling over the fire, she thought back over the weeks they had lived with the hill folk. *Thank you, Jesus, for these kind people.*

When breakfast ended, Margaret and Agnes cleaned the wooden bowls and horn spoons. As Margaret returned them to their makeshift shelf, she noticed that only three bannocks and about a quart of meal remained. *What will our friends eat when this is gone?* she wondered.

Thomas was waiting when they finished their work. They returned to their sleeping quarters, put on all of their clothing, and picked up their bedrolls. *Human sausages again*, Margaret thought with a wry smile. The group knelt to ask for safe travel. Then the men shook hands with Thomas, and one by one the women hugged Agnes and Margaret. Jonathan's wife thrust a small bundle into Margaret's hand. Margaret could tell from its shape what was inside. She shook her head.

The woman nodded toward Agnes and whispered, "For her."

Margaret hesitated. How could she accept the last three bannocks when there was little meal to make any more? She opened her mouth to protest the gift but closed it when the woman raised her forefinger to her lips and smiled.

"We must go," Jonathan said.

"May God protect you," someone called after them as they waved good-bye.

They had not gone far when Margaret, who was walking behind the others, turned around and raced back to the cave. She glanced around. No one was in sight. Slipping up to the entrance, she placed the package containing two of the bannocks where they were sure to be found. Her mission completed, she scurried back to join the others. Jonathan looked at her sternly but held his peace.

Light snow began to fall, and the girls pulled their shawls tighter around their heads. The first hour of the journey they tramped through familiar territory. Margaret's feet were cold, and the frost nipped at her nose and her fingers. She glanced at Agnes. Her lips were set with that determined look she had whenever she faced a challenge. So far she hadn't become ill, but it was still a long time until spring. For Agnes's sake Margaret hoped their new hidey hole would be warm. The girl was so thin, and she often coughed. *I promised to take care of her. Was it wrong to bring her with us?* The question chilled Margaret as deeply as the cold that seeped through her cloak and boots. But another part of her argued, *You prayed for wisdom and then did what the Lord led you to do. No turning back!*

Jonathan stopped frequently so Agnes could rest. At midday they paused by a burn and enjoyed a drink from its icy waters. Margaret drew out the lone bannock and insisted that Agnes eat all of it.

Midafternoon they entered a dense thicket. "We have to climb a hill," Jonathan said. Thomas and Margaret grasped Agnes's hands and helped her up the steepest parts. At the top, they stopped, waiting for her breathing to return to normal.

When it appeared they were rested, Jonathan took Thomas's hand. "We need to hold on to one another," he said. "We're going down the other side, and it's much steeper."

Margaret stared at the snow-covered slope they were about to descend. "Hold on tight," she said to Agnes, leading her toward the edge. "It looks quite slipper—" Before she could finish her sentence, she lost her footing. Down the hill she slid with Agnes clinging to her like a second skin.

23
SECRET WINTER REFUGE

Margaret and Agnes landed in a heap at the bottom of the steep hill, their fall cushioned by a snow drift. They untangled themselves and waited for Jonathan and Thomas to pick their way down. Grateful that they were not injured by their sudden flight down the slope, Margaret stood and looked at her surroundings. They appeared to be in a secluded hollow.

"This way," Jonathan said as he dropped Thomas's hand. "It's not far. Just to the left and under the hill." In a few minutes they came upon an abandoned steading.

Thomas surveyed the weathered farmhouse and the byre, now overgrown with hawthorns. "It doesn't look like anyone has lived here in years."

A hint of a smile lit Jonathan's face as he led them into the crudely furnished house.

Grateful to be indoors after living in the cave for two weeks, Margaret checked out the kitchen area. "Look," she said, pointing to a kist standing in a corner near a generous pile of firewood and clumps of peat. After opening the kist, she exclaimed, "There's enough meal for several weeks!" She held up a handful of kail. "And look at this!" She turned her puzzled eyes to Jonathan. "Where did this food come from? Whose house is this? Why was it abandoned?"

"One question at a time, please," Jonathan said. "The house was abandoned many years ago. We have been using it for several years."

Thomas frowned. "Are we . . . are we really, um, safe here?"

"Of course. This is one of the safest places we've found."

"Then why did you bring *us* here?" Margaret asked. "Why didn't the people who stayed here last winter come back?" When Jonathan did not respond immediately, she glanced up. A look of anguish covered his face.

"Some of us are called to endure for years," he said. "Others receive their rewards much sooner."

Margaret dared not ask any more in front of Agnes. But she wondered if Jonathan was holding back something he didn't want them to know. *Why did he bring us here?* Aloud she said, "Other Covenanters are more important than we are."

"We're all important in the Lord's eyes," Jonathan replied. "He has a plan for each of us." He inhaled deeply and drew back his shoulders. "Sometimes we don't understand what it is. But we study his word to find out, and we do our best to do what we think he wants."

Margaret was still puzzled. Why should the three of them be given the safest place? Didn't Jonathan trust them? Without realizing it, she anxiously chewed her lower lip. She stopped when she saw Jonathan staring at her. Then he spoke again, but with hesitation. "I didn't plan to tell you this, but . . ." He looked from one to the other and said softly, "There is a price on your heads."

Agnes shuddered, and Margaret pulled her close. Thomas's mouth flew open. "On us? Why?"

"We are living in the killing times," Jonathan said, as though the words were being wrung out of him. "Time tries all as winter tries the kail," he added as though speaking to himself. "When we suffer hardships in life, we come through them better able to serve the Lord."

The killing times. Jonathan's words pierced Margaret's heart. Lady Stewart had used the same ones. Now the shadow of death seemed to pass over Margaret as they stood shivering in their new hiding place.

"Some of our friends are weak in their faith. They fear the persecutors. They give in to the demands of the king's dragoons," Jonathan continued in a strained voice. "Things have gotten worse since you left Glenvernoch. The dragoons are determined to track down every last one of us." He lowered his voice. "Unfortunately they are succeeding."

Agnes slid closer to her sister, and Thomas scowled. Margaret was glad Fergus had fled to Drumjargon before things got so bad. *Please, Lord, protect him*, she prayed. *And us.*

"Neighbors are forced to spy on neighbors," Jonathan said. "Soldiers offer money to anyone who can tell them where we are. We needed to put you in a safe place because finding the three of you would be quite profitable."

Margaret felt her throat tighten. "But not everyone is disloyal," Jonathan said, and his face softened. "We still have fearless sympathizers like Widow M'Lauchlan. They own the covenant, and they stand up for what the Bible teaches."

At the mention of Widow M'Lauchlan, Margaret and Agnes gasped. "Widow M'Lauchlan is our friend," Margaret said.

Jonathan nodded. "She is friend to all Covenanters. People like her provide the food here in this farmhouse. Day after day they risk their lives to help us survive." He looked at Thomas. "You must learn your way around. Go out each day, but be careful not to show yourself. Look everywhere for bundles or baskets of provisions."

"We're grateful to you for bringing us here," Margaret said.

"Aye," said Thomas. "Thank you for welcoming us on the moors. You have been so kind. But you've never told us your last name."

"No, and I am not going to." He pulled his jacket tighter as if he were about to leave. "The dragoons torture women and children to learn the names of their Covenanting friends." He looked Thomas in the eye and said, "Jonathan is not my real name. It is best you don't know what it is. What you don't know, you can't tell."

Jonathan turned toward the stone hearth where a fire had been laid with dried bracken and small twigs from dead tree branches. He looked about the hearth until he spotted a steel rod and a piece of flint. After laying the flint on the stone fireplace, he knelt and struck it deftly, sending a shower of tiny sparks into the twigs and bracken. He learned forward and blew gently, nursing the sparks into a blaze. When it appeared the fire was strong enough that it wouldn't burn itself out, he added a small clump of peat. Rising, he turned to his young friends. "I've told you much more than I intended to. And now I must go."

Icy fingers of fear crept up Margaret's spine. Jonathan, or whoever he was, was about to leave them alone in this strange place. She didn't want him to go. "Surely you won't walk back to the cave tonight?" she said.

"We have friends all over Galloway," Jonathan said. "I will stay the night with one of them." He sighed, but he sounded content. "I will sleep in a warm bed and enjoy a good breakfast. In the morning, I will find out what has happened the past few weeks." He shook hands with Thomas. "God bless you all," he said. And then he was gone.

The three stared at the door long after it closed behind him. Then Thomas knelt down to encourage the fire. The girls gathered near, letting its blaze warm their hearts as well as their bodies. From now on they must guard the flame carefully so that it never went completely out.

Margaret wished she knew how to start a fire from flint and steel. She wondered if Thomas could do it. She went to the larder and returned with some kail. She set a pot of water to heating on the hearth and added a bit of salt from the supply she had found near the kist. *Thank you, Lord, for the salt.* Agnes discovered some oatcakes on a shelf. She put them on the table and sat down by the fire while Margaret waited for the pot to boil. Before long she nodded off. Margaret awakened her when the meal was ready.

The weary young people were too tired to talk as they ate their kail and oatcakes. When their supper was over, Margaret suggested that Agnes sleep in the box bed across the room from the fire. Sleepy and still cold, Agnes crawled into bed. Margaret tucked her blanket around her and kissed her good night. Thomas smothered the glowing embers with loose peat dust—to keep enough heat through the night that could be puffed into life in the morning. Then he and Margaret wrapped themselves in their blankets and lay down in front of the hearth. Margaret heard Thomas getting up several times during the night to check on the fire. If Agnes coughed, she did not hear it.

Margaret awakened the next morning to a glowing fire that Thomas had stirred up. She hadn't slept in such a warm place since they left Glenvernoch. She looked around and thanked the Lord for their new hidey hole. It was a pleasure to get up and prepare breakfast. Afterwards she would heat water so she and Agnes could wash themselves near the warmth of the fireplace.

As they ate, Thomas presented his plans for learning his way around. "Each day I'll explore a little farther than the previous one."

"You must be careful not to be seen," Margaret cautioned. "Or to get lost."

"I'll follow my own footprints in the snow while I am still in the hollow. When I leave it, I'll choose landmarks to help me find my way."

They finished their meal, and Thomas pulled his jacket tighter. "We'll be praying for you," Margaret said. "You won't go far today, will you?"

"Not today. I want to see what's in the old barn." With that he was out the door, closing it softly behind him.

"Let's clear the table and talk with the Lord," Margaret suggested. "Then we'll see what we can find inside this house."

On their second day at the farmhouse, Thomas decided to climb the hill. "I'll take my snare with me," he said. "Maybe the Lord will send a hare across my path."

The very thought of meat in their broth made Margaret smile.

Echoing Margaret's thoughts, Agnes said, "A hare would taste so good! We could use its fur, too."

"Thomas, be careful," Margaret said as her brother picked up the snare.

"I will," he promised.

Aye, Lord. Please help Thomas to be careful. And to find a hare today.

The hares weren't out on the ridge that day, but Thomas returned with a basket full of oatcakes, bannocks, and kail. "We must be fairly close to some village where the people are sympathetic to Covenanters," he said.

Agnes pulled an oatcake from the basket. "I'm glad strangers leave us food."

Thomas looked at Margaret. "Maybe it's a family from Wigtown who is helping us."

Margaret blinked in surprise. "Are we *that* close to Wigtown?"

A hint of mischief sparkled in Thomas's eyes. "I think so. And that means we're not far from Drumjargon either."

At the mention of Drumjargon, Margaret dropped the kail she was carrying to the larder. How she wished she could see Fergus again. A look of quiet understanding passed between her and Thomas. She scooped up the kail and set it on the table.

"Some morning I'm going to go to Wigtown and see if I can find out anything about Father."

Agnes's eyes brightened. "Do you think you could?"

"I hope so."

Margaret shot a glance in Thomas's direction, a silent message that asked, "Won't that be quite risky?"

The next two days were too snowy for Thomas to go exploring. Margaret felt safe in their hidey hole in the hollow, and she thought Agnes did, too. Still, there was the nagging concern about their food supply. There was enough meal to last for a few weeks, but she didn't know how long they'd be staying in the farmhouse. *Lord, please help Thomas find a basket of food tomorrow,* she prayed as she set about heating water to wash some of their clothing.

The following morning, Margaret and Agnes awakened before Thomas. Agnes opened the tiny shutters and peered out. "Wake up, Thomas," she said. "Today you can go out again."

Thomas rolled over and stretched. "Good," he said as he unwrapped himself from his bedroll. "Now that the snow has stopped, the hares are likely to come out of their hiding places." He pulled on his boots. "Ask the Lord to help me catch one today."

Margaret nodded as she heated water to cook breakfast, but she couldn't stop worrying. What if Thomas didn't catch a hare today? Or tomorrow? What if he got lost? Or what if he got found . . . by a dragoon? *Lord, quiet my heart and mind,* she prayed. *Only you can.*

24

AN OUTDOOR ADVENTURE

As Agnes cleared away the breakfast table, Margaret noted her quick, light steps. Gone was the weary tread that brought her to this hidey hole. *She's stronger now that we are living indoors*, Margaret observed. "Let's read some of the verses Fergus gave me," Margaret said. "Then I have a nice surprise for afterwards."

They sat down by the fire, and Margaret pulled out the precious paper covered with Fergus's tiny handwriting. After reading several chapters, she asked Agnes what she'd like to sing.

"Let's sing the psalm about our hiding place this morning," Agnes said. "I love it."

"So do I. Especially verses seven and eight." The sisters joined their voices in the familiar verses.

> Thou art my hiding place, thou shalt
> from trouble keep me free;
> Thou with songs of deliverance
> about shalt compass me.

I will instruct thee, and thee teach
the way that thou shalt go;
And, with mine eye upon thee set.
I will direction show.

"Jesus really is our hiding place, isn't he, Meggie?"

"Aye, sister. He's protected us through our wanderings. He holds us in the palm of his hand, and he'll never let go." She paused, thinking about their unknown future. "The Lord's brought us safely to this old house. No matter what happens, we can trust him to watch over us today and every day."

The girls knelt to pray. "Thank you, Jesus, for keeping us safe," Agnes prayed. "Please protect Thomas. Watch over Mother and Father." Her voice faltered. "Help them know how much we love them."

As Agnes sniffed away her tears, Margaret prayed for their friends in hiding throughout Galloway. "Lord, please end the persecution so we can return home."

Rising from her knees, Margaret said, "We've been shut in far too long. Let's bundle up and go outside. We can walk to the far end of the clearing." She inhaled deeply as if already enjoying the fresh air. "Thomas says there is a stand of rowan trees just around the curve in the hillside. I can't wait to feel the sun on my face."

Agnes frowned. "I don't want to go outside."

"Is it too far for you to walk?" When Agnes didn't respond, Margaret looked her way. Agnes's eyes were dark with fear. Margaret reached out and pulled her close. "Don't be afraid," she said, gently stroking her back. "You can't see the trees from the top of the hill. Thomas checked that out our first day here." She smiled as she massaged her sister's thin back.

"Jonathan said only the oldest citizens in the shire remember this deserted steading. Since you can't see it from the top of the hill, it's been forgotten."

"All right, then," Agnes said. "I was scared that someone might see us."

"It will feel good to get outside, won't it?" Margaret added a few clumps of peat to the fire. "We'll be like your orphaned lambs last spring." They pulled on their boots. "Remember how they scampered about when we turned them loose after feeding them in the house for so long?"

Agnes giggled. "I loved the way they twitched their stubby little tails."

"I liked their wooly fleece," Margaret added. She dropped the subject when she remembered it would soon be lambing time in Glenvernoch. She must not upset Agnes with reminders of home.

Outside, Margaret sighed with pleasure at the beauty of the sparkling snow that blanketed the narrow hollow. "I was beginning to feel like a prisoner," she said. Her thoughts wandered back a week to their first days in the old farmhouse. At first she had been fearful, but her apprehension subsided on the second day when Thomas returned with a basket of provisions. She was surprised to learn they were near Wigtown. She wondered when he'd try to go there. She hoped it would be soon. Breathing in the refreshing air helped her forget, at least for the moment, that they were among the hunted. A question from Agnes brought her wandering thoughts back to the hollow.

"Do you think Thomas will go to Wigtown today?"

"Perhaps. It would be wonderful if he returned with news."
Especially news from Mother and Father.

"I wish we could go to Wigtown with him," Agnes said, her voice filled with longing. "Or home," she whispered, "but I know it's not safe to do that."

"I would like to go to Drumjargon to see Widow M'Lauchlan." She wondered how things were going with her. She'd taught her so much about being brave. His Royal Highness's dragoons didn't scare the widow. *If only I could be more like her.*

"I wish I were as brave as she is," Agnes said.

"That's just what I was thinking!" said Margaret. "Jesus will give us courage when we need it."

Widow M'Lauchlan wasn't the only person drawing her to Drumjargon. *Dear Fergus. I wish I could see him again.* Her eyes misted with longing for what might have been.

As they crossed the clearing, the girls talked about their hill friends now scattered for the winter. Margaret prayed that they all were safe. They were almost to the rowan trees when Agnes asked, "Why are you smiling?"

"Am I?"

"Aye. What makes you so happy?"

"Lots of things. For one thing, being out in this sunshine!" There was a long pause. Agnes glanced in her direction. Margaret sighed and then added, "Drumjargon is not far from Wigtown. I was also thinking about Fergus Walker."

"You miss him, don't you?" When Margaret nodded without saying any more, Agnes spoke again. "He was more than just a friend, wasn't he?"

"Aye," Margaret whispered. "He was." She needed to change the subject. "We have another reason to smile," she said. "We're close to Wigtown and the dragoons don't know it, even though we're almost under their noses. God is protecting us."

At the mention of the dragoons, Agnes tensed. Her lower lip began to tremble.

"The Lord has kept us safe thus far, Aggie. Nothing will happen to us that he doesn't allow. He will help us face whatever evils come upon us. Our job is to be faithful."

"But what if the dragoons find us?" Agnes shuddered. "Jonathan said there's a reward for anyone who tells them where we are."

"Aye," said Margaret, "but the Lord will still be with us." She put her arms around her trembling sister. "Jesus promised us the crown of life," she said softly. "That's our reward for being faithful, even when our lives are threatened."

"I want to be faithful, but I'm s-scared of being caught— and tortured. Or . . . of . . . being . . . killed," she whispered.

Margaret held her closer. *Dear God, please help me be brave for Agnes's sake as well as for my own.* "Even if we face death, Jesus will be with us. He will give us boldness before our enemies."

"How do you know that?" Agnes whispered.

"Because of Covenanters like Donald Cargill. When he was led to the gallows, he knew Jesus was waiting to receive him in heaven." She paused long, considering the kind of welcome the Lord must have given such a faithful man. "He was fearless because he knew he would soon see the Lord face to face." She searched for words to comfort her sister. "Because Mr. Cargill loved Jesus so much, he was glad to leave his troubles behind and go to live with him in heaven." Margaret glanced at Agnes.

Agnes returned her glance. "Being in heaven with Jesus would be nicer than having to run from the dragoons."

"Aye," Margaret said, her voice thick with feeling. "Aggie, the king's soldiers may kill our bodies. But they cannot touch

our souls. Jesus will give us whatever we need in our trials."
She reached out and took her sister's hand. "Let's enjoy the
sunshine while we can." She looked around. "See," she said,
pointing ahead toward the trees, "we're almost to the other
side of the clearing. Now, aren't you glad we came?"

Before Agnes could answer, the air was split by the sounds
of lapwings. The birds must have been wintering in the sheltered valley. "Pee-ee-wit. Pee-ee-wit," they called as they
darted into the air and then circled back down before rising
again. Their wings glistened in the sunlight as they gyrated
above the trees.

"They're beautiful!" Agnes said. "I'm sorry we disturbed
them."

Margaret winced as though she'd received a big fist in
her stomach. She grabbed Agnes by the arm and shoved her
under the trees where she hoped they were completely hidden.
"Aggie," she said, trying to speak calmly. "You don't understand.
Lapwings leave their nests when they are disturbed. That's
how the dragoons found some of the hill folk."

Margaret struggled to control her fears. If there were dragoons in the area, they'd suspect someone was down here in
the hollow and investigate. *Please, God, may there be nobody near
enough to hear the birds.* She prayed silently lest Agnes become
more frightened. The girls huddled down between two snow
drifts with the trees standing over them like guardians. Minutes passed like hours, and Agnes began to shake from the
cold. They must get back to the farmhouse. She took Agnes's
hand and stood. "Jesus, protect us," she said and then pulled
Aggie up. They dashed across the snowy hollow, back to the
safety of the old house, slammed the door behind them, and
knelt to thank the Lord for his protection.

After eating a bowl of warm gruel, the girls fell asleep bathed in the warmth from the smoldering hearth. They were awakened by the sound of Thomas returning to the farmhouse. His eyes widened as Agnes told him about their walk and the lapwings' alarm. "God is good to us!" he said. "Now let me tell you about my day."

25

No Hare, but—

"I didn't even see any tracks today," Thomas said when he returned. "After wandering about for what seemed like hours, I came upon a familiar path, but I couldn't remember where it led." He scratched his head. "Maybe it was the snow covering that confused me. Anyway, I decided to follow it."

"Where did it end?" Margaret asked.

Thomas smiled, prolonging the suspense a few more seconds. "In Wigtown!"

"So you were right about our being near the burgh," Margaret said.

Thomas nodded and grinned at her. "I recognized the huge oak just outside Wigtown, where the path runs south to Drumjargon."

Margaret stared at her brother as though he were the angel Gabriel. They were close to Wigtown and Drumjargon—to Widow M'Lauchlan and Fergus Walker.

"It's been a tiring day," Thomas said. "Perhaps we should all go to bed." He added wood to keep the fire alive through the night.

Before long Thomas and Margaret could hear Agnes's rhythmic breathing in her box bed as they lay wrapped in their blankets near the hearth. When Margaret was certain Agnes was asleep, she nudged Thomas. "We need to talk," she whispered.

Thomas turned in his blanket and leaned on an elbow. "Talk? Now? Can't it wait until morning?"

"No. I need to discuss something without telling Agnes."

Thomas was wider awake now. "What?"

"I want to go to Drumjargon," she whispered.

"You *what?*" Thomas bolted into a sitting position.

"Shhh!" Margaret warned. "Don't wake Agnes. She would want to go with me, and I don't think that's a good idea."

"It isn't a good idea. For her or for you. Why do you want to go there?"

"To see Widow M'Lauchlan. She always knows what's going on with us Covenanters. Maybe she can tell us something about Mother and Father, too."

"You cannot go there. It would be dangerous for both of you!"

Though she was two years older than Thomas, Margaret usually agreed with him. This time his words fell on deaf ears. "I know it's dangerous. That is why I need to go alone. If I get caught, Agnes will be safe here with you."

"Margaret, there's a price on our heads!" His sister remained silent, her signal that she would not give in. Thomas got up to add a few more sticks of wood to the fire. "Can we talk about it tomorrow?"

As he watched, Margaret pulled her blanket tighter around her feet, turned over, and went to sleep.

For the next few days, life in the abandoned farmhouse continued with the same dull routine. Thomas left after breakfast each morning to search for food and explore the territory around their hiding place. Margaret chafed at not being able to talk with him privately. Finally her patience wore out. "Aggie," she said one morning after he left them for the day. "I'm going to Drumjargon. Maybe I can find out something about Mother and Father."

Aggie looked at her as though she were a stranger. Finally, she found her voice. "You can't, Meggie! It isn't safe."

Margaret returned her stare. "The only safe place is in the Lord's keeping," she said. "I trust him to get me to Widow M'Lauchlan's home. I have to find out what has happened to Mother and Father."

Tears filled Agnes's eyes. "I miss them so much."

"So do I," Margaret said as she pulled her sister close. She could feel Agnes's heart beating . . . fast. She needed to leave before she lost her courage. Thank goodness Thomas had told her how to find the trail to Wigtown.

"I'll follow Thomas's footprints up the hill. I should be back by the time he returns." She looked into her sister's eyes. "Are you afraid to stay alone?"

"No," Agnes said, though it sounded like she was trying to convince herself.

"Then, I'm going," Margaret said, grabbing her cloak. "Pray that I get to Drumjargon without any trouble." She left quickly before Agnes could change her mind and call her back.

26

MARGARET GOES EXPLORING

Margaret had considered going to Wigtown for news, but she knew no one there. If she went to Drumjargon, she could visit Widow M'Lauchlan. Maybe she'd see Fergus again. It hadn't snowed for a week, and the weather had remained cold, so it was easy to follow Thomas's footprints. When she came to the path that led south, she chose it. After checking to make sure no one was about, she crept past the kailyard lined with currant bushes to Widow M'Lauchlan's door. She knocked lightly. When the door opened, she found herself face to face with the wispy old lady who had first told her about the Covenanters.

The widow's deep-set eyes registered shock. "Margaret?" She pulled her thin, disheveled guest into her cottage and closed the door. Then she hugged her so tight it left them both breathless. "I never thought to see you again," she said through tear-filled eyes. She clutched the hem of her apron and glanced toward the door. "I hope no one saw you come here."

"I was careful," Margaret assured her.

Widow M'Lauchlan sighed. "The dragoons are always sneaking around my cottage. They're hoping I'll do something they say is wrong so they can report me to Grierson—or Provost Coltrane." A smug smile lit her face. "They have been spying on me ever since the Lord called my husband home."

She motioned for Margaret to sit by the hearth and then knelt to stir up the fire. She pulled a pot forward where it soon began to bubble joyously. Before long the aroma of kail boiling in beef broth filled the little farmhouse, reminding Margaret of Mother and home. She blinked and swallowed to keep from drooling. Widow M'Lauchlan set a steaming bowl before her and urged her to eat. As Margaret picked up her spoon, the widow questioned her about her visit. "By coming here, you risked being caught by the dragoons. Where did you come from? What do you want from me?"

Between bites of tasty stew, Margaret told her where she and her sister and Thomas were hiding. "It's been difficult, but the Lord is with us." Widow M'Lauchlan nodded. "Strangers leave food and warm clothing where we find them. But," she swallowed to help her words get by the lump growing in her throat, "we've had no word from Mother and Father since we left home in early February."

Widow M'Lauchlan reached out and grasped her hands. "If only we knew how things were with them," Margaret whispered. "Do you know?"

"I know a little about their situation."

Margaret sat up straighter. She didn't want to miss a word.

"Your family is well known. So is the commitment of you young people. It is a dubious honor to have a price on your heads." She squeezed Margaret's hands and looked into her eyes as though she were demanding a promise. "I pray you'll always keep your covenant." She paused. "Now I'll tell you what I know."

Speaking in a soft, controlled voice, Widow M'Lauchlan said, "The dragoons have spoiled the farmhouse. They've eaten the livestock—or driven it off."

"No! Not Father's prized sheep and cattle!"

Margaret's anguished outburst closed Widow M'Lauchlan's mouth. But Margaret insisted she go on. "I won't leave until you tell me everything!"

Widow M'Lauchlan shook her head. Laying a comforting hand on Margaret's shoulder, she said, "Because you three no longer attend kirk, the minister has listed you as disorderly parishioners. Your father must ride to the tolbooth in Wigtown every Friday to pay a ridiculous fine for each Lord's Day you are absent."

Margaret bowed her head in sorrow. She must never let Agnes know the price Mother and Father were paying because they'd run away. She fought to hold back her sobs. Then something Widow M'Lauchlan had said brought a ray of hope. "Father rides to Wigtown every week?"

"Aye, and 'tis a pity that he must. It is a long journey in winter, even on his strong horse." She sighed as though she, too, shared Margaret's anguish. "The fines have ruined him."

"I wish I could see him and Mother." Margaret blinked. "Is my mother well?"

Widow M'Lauchlan raised her shoulders in a gesture of unknowing. "I'm sorry, Margaret. I've heard nothing about Mrs. Wilson." She looked at her sharply. "You might be able to see your father when he comes to Wigtown." She paused and added, "It would be dangerous—but so is your visit here today."

As Margaret tried to find her voice, the widow spoke again. "I have more news. The king is dead."

Margaret sputtered. "Dead? His Royal Highness is dead? When did he die? What happened to him?"

"On the sixth of February," Widow M'Lauchlan said. "He had a stroke. Then other ills befell him."

"Now we can go home!"

"Oh, no!" Widow M'Lauchlan responded. "There is still a price on your heads! We hope the new King James will repeal those cruel laws enacted against us, or at least ignore them. Until he does, our lives are still in danger." She waited for Margaret to regain her composure. "You must remember it is very dangerous for any of you to be seen in Wigtown." She gave Margaret a motherly hug. "I want to give you some food. Then you must leave. We would both be in trouble if the dragoons found you here."

Widow M'Lauchlan filled a bag with kail and oats and six thick bannocks. "You can enjoy a hearty supper tonight," she said.

Margaret thanked her and bowed her head as the widow prayed for her and her family. Then she led her across the room and out a hidden door known only to her Covenanter friends. "May the Lord continue to protect you," she said as she waved good-bye.

27

SHARING THE NEWS

Margaret crept back to the main trail and onto the ridge above the old farmhouse. Elated at being the bearer of good news, she hunkered down on her haunches and slid down the steep bank. She hit the bottom with a bone-rattling *whomp!* Lying in a heap in the snow, she waited for her thumping heart to settle down. Then she picked up the bag of food and headed toward their refuge under the hill.

Thomas was already home. One glance at him and she knew how worried he'd been. "Margaret!" he whispered as he grabbed her and hugged her tight. "Thank God you're home." Agnes rushed forward and clung to her as though she'd never let go.

Silence blanketed the farmhouse like a heavy storm cloud, broken only by the crackling of the fire in the hearth. Minutes passed before anyone could speak. During that interval Margaret and Thomas exchanged glances over Agnes's head. They'd call a truce about her leaving until they could discuss it alone.

When Margaret's voice was steady enough not to betray her, she said, "I have something for you." She picked up the poke of food and handed it to Agnes.

Thomas moved closer to his sister as she opened the bag and pulled out the thickest bannock they had ever seen. Agnes's eyes widened when she retrieved five more, as fat as the first one. Finally she pulled out enough kail to make many suppers. "Where did you get these things?" she asked.

"From Widow M'Lauchlan," Margaret said.

Thomas's jaw dropped. "You went to Drumjargon?"

Margaret nodded. "We had a pleasant visit. Widow M'Lauchlan's cottage smelled just like home when Mother bakes bannocks."

Though he said nothing, Thomas blanched at the risks she'd taken.

"Widow M'Lauchlan insisted I eat a bowl of warm broth. As I sat at her table, she told me some news." Thomas's eyes widened. "As I bid her good-bye, she handed me this food. She said we should keep trusting Jes—"

"News?" Thomas interrupted.

"News of Mother? And Father?" Agnes asked, her voice aquiver.

Margaret weighed her words carefully. "Widow M'Lauchlan didn't have any news about Mother."

Disappointed, Agnes wiped her eyes. Thomas looked at Margaret with concern. "What about Father? What did she say about him?"

"Father is forced to go to Wigtown every week."

Thomas frowned. "To Wigtown? Why? It's not time for any of the fairs. Or the season to take his wool to market."

Margaret hesitated to answer, but neither Thomas nor Agnes would be put off. "Is Father in trouble because we ran away?" Agnes asked.

Margaret spoke with as much control as she could muster. "Every Friday he must go to the burgh court. In the tolbooth. He has to pay a fine each time we're absent from kirk."

Thomas grimaced as though he had a fierce stomachache. But Agnes's face brightened. "Why don't we go to Wigtown to see him?" she blurted out.

Thomas shook his head. "Aggie," he said, "we cannot go anywhere. There's a price on our heads." He looked as if he wanted to cry. "Friends are bribed or tortured to inform against each other. Like Jesus, we would be betrayed in exchange for a few coins."

Thomas had spoken the truth. Still, Margaret tucked her thoughts about slipping off to Wigtown into a corner of her mind to be retrieved later. "I've more news," she said.

"I hope it's better than what you've just told us," Thomas muttered.

"His Royal Highness is dead."

"Dead? The wicked king is dead?" Thomas's voice sounded hollow.

"Aye," Margaret said, "There is a new King James. Nobody knows what that means to us." She chewed her lower lip. "Widow M'Lauchlan says the persecution has died down a wee bit."

"We'll stay hidden until we know how this new king feels about Covenanters," Thomas said. He got up to tend the fire. "We are all tired and hungry. Let's eat some of that fine food Widow M'Lauchlan sent home for us."

Margaret put a kettle of water over the fire for the kail, and Agnes set the table. While the kail boiled, they rested. Then they ate in silence, each lost in private thoughts.

When Thomas finished eating, he said, "I think it's time we went to our beds." His weary sisters nodded in agreement. Thomas rolled himself into his blanket in front of the hearth.

Margaret followed Agnes to her box bed on the opposite side of the room. Keeping her back toward Thomas, she whispered, "I'm going to Wigtown to try to see Father."

"But, Meggie, Thomas says it's too dangerous."

"I know it's dangerous," Margaret whispered, "but I'm still going." Usually Margaret respected her brother's opinions. But this time her desire to see her father overruled her common sense. *I must see him and find out about Mother.*

Agnes touched her arm. "Meggie, let's go to Wigtown together," she said. "We can ask the Lord to protect us and to help us find Father."

"No, Agnes, you must stay here where it's safe," Margaret said.

"Please, Meggie, promise you won't go without me," Agnes whispered, on the verge of tears.

Margaret hesitated. Then, fearing Agnes would try to follow her if she left alone, she said, "I promise. But we'd better not tell Thomas. Now let's go to sleep. We'll talk about it in the morning after he goes off for the day."

Margaret shut her eyes, but her mind kept working. She didn't like the idea of not telling Thomas. Perhaps it would be best if they all went to Wigtown. She would at least ask him. Her decision made, she rolled over, snuggled down into her blanket, and slept.

The next morning, Margaret blurted out their plan to go to Wigtown. Thomas's horn spoon crashed into his bowl. A look of horrified disbelief spread over his face.

"Are you daft, Margaret?"

Margaret gazed at him, willing him to understand why she had to go. "You could go with us."

"If the three of us showed up in Wigtown, we would be recognized in a trice," Thomas replied, "and reported to the dragoons."

"Thomas," said Margaret, "this might be our only chance to see Father."

"Couldn't we slip into Wigtown just like Margaret did in Drumjargon?" Agnes asked. "The Lord protected her yesterday. Can't he protect us again?"

After what seemed a very long time, Thomas spoke in a deflated voice. "This is a dangerous idea. You would have to hang around the magistrate's office to watch for Father. When you did that—" His voice died out.

Thomas was right. She was putting them all at risk by insisting on going to the tolbooth. She wished she hadn't promised to take Agnes. It would be easier to slip into Wigtown alone. "Please, Thomas, we need you to go with us."

Thomas sighed and raked his fingers through his hair. "Let's pray about it for a few days. If you still feel it is the Lord's will, I'll go as far as the big oak tree just outside the village." He looked from his sisters to the thick bannocks Margaret had brought home. "Save three of them to take with us . . . if we decide to go."

Margaret smiled at Agnes and gave Thomas a hug. "Thank you," she said. *Saving the bannocks is a good omen.*

For the next few days, life in the old farmhouse continued with the same monotonous routine. They prayed daily for protection and for direction, especially about going to Wigtown. Thomas went off each morning hoping to catch a hare or find food left for them. Meanwhile, Margaret grew impatient.

After almost a week, Thomas said, "We will go to Wigtown tomorrow. I'll take you to the outskirts in a roundabout way. That makes the trip longer but safer. I'll wait at the edge of the village while you slip in to watch for Father. Once you've seen him, ask him to return with you. I'll pray for you and wait for your return."

Margaret grabbed her sister's hands, and the girls skipped around the room, their happiness having traveled from their hearts to their feet.

"Now I must be on my way," Thomas said, grabbing his jacket and his snare. "Pray that the Lord sends some food today. Boiled hare would make a hearty supper before we begin our journey."

"We will," Agnes said, as the door closed behind him. *Aye*, Margaret thought. She would pray harder than she'd ever prayed before. She had already caused her family to suffer severely. She didn't want to grieve them any more. Fergus's father was right. It *was* hard to own the covenant.

28

REUNION IN WIGTOWN

The brisk March morning had scarcely dawned when Margaret arose to prepare breakfast. Thomas had already stirred up the fire, so it didn't take long to warm the water. An atmosphere of anticipation and fear filled the room.

Once they finished breakfast, Thomas led them in prayer. "Please watch over us today," he said. "Help my sisters to find Father in Wigtown." His voice choked with emotion. After clearing his throat, he continued. "We thank you for keeping us safe ever since we left home. Thank you for friends who have shared their food and lodging."

Agnes washed their bowls, and Thomas added more wood to the fire to keep it smoldering while they were gone. They pulled on their boots and their heaviest clothing. Then Thomas led the way across the clearing, and they began the slow climb up the steep slope of the snow-covered hill.

Several hours later, they came to the big oak, standing like a sentinel at the outskirts of Wigtown. Thomas pointed out the route to the magistrate's office. "That is Main Street right ahead of us," he said. "It will take you to the tolbooth where Father comes to pay the fines. You'll recognize it by the tall tower. You must be very careful," he warned. "Pull your shawls over your heads and walk briskly past the tolbooth as if you're on an errand. When you get to the end of the street, turn around and walk back slowly. Do not do anything to attract attention."

His brow furrowed as he continued. "Men will be heading to the tolbooth to do business. Watch who goes in and out. Keep your eyes and ears open, but don't talk." He hugged his sisters. "I will wait right here. Once you see Father, don't linger. You must not look suspicious leaving Wigtown."

Agnes seized Margaret's hand and held it tightly as they headed into the village. "If God wills it, we will see Father soon," Margaret said. Under her breath she prayed. *Jesus, I'm afraid. Protect us. Help us find Father.* She paused and then added, *And, Lord, we'll love you even if we don't find him.*

Having been in Wigtown with their father when he brought his wool to market, the girls had no difficulty in finding the impressive old tolbooth. As they approached it, a number of men were going in and out, just as Thomas said.

Margaret shuddered at the thought of those who had been hanged in front of the tolbooth. Next door stood a small jail house. Most of the time it overflowed with Covenanters facing trial and sentencing. Widow M'Lauchlan had told her that when the jail could hold no more, captives were flung into a dark coal cellar across the street, near Provost Coltrane's house. Someone had once referred to it as Thieves' Hole. The name had stuck. Those who were imprisoned there endured the inky darkness and were sometimes forgotten.

Margaret wondered if the prisoners were fed or even given a light in the darkness. Taking her sister's hand once more, she realized Agnes's pulse was beating as rapidly as her own. They had not seen their father for nearly two months. Would today be the day they'd see him again?

The girls turned at the end of the street and headed back toward the tolbooth. They were almost to the magistrate's office when Margaret stopped abruptly. "Look," she gasped. In the distance, their father headed toward them. He walked with his head bowed low and his shoulders stooped.

"Where's his horse?" Agnes said and then started forward.

Margaret grabbed her sister with both hands to prevent her from running to him. "No," she whispered. "We must wait until he comes out of the office. Then we will follow him quietly until we catch up with him."

Father disappeared inside, and the girls slowed their pace as much as they dared. A man about the age of their oldest brother stopped them. "Are you looking for the magistrate?" he asked in a voice that was neither kind nor sympathetic.

"Oh, no," Margaret said, thrusting her sweaty palms deeper into the folds of her cloak. "It's such a lovely day, we're out enjoying the sunshine." She smiled, hoping to put him off.

Without another word, the stranger turned and disappeared inside. Margaret held her breath until he was out of sight. "That man frightened me," Agnes whispered.

His presence had disturbed Margaret, too, but she wouldn't let Agnes know that. "Come on," she said. "Let's go by the office once more to show we really are walking just for pleasure." She took Agnes by the arm and headed toward the tolbooth. They hadn't walked more than three paces when the door opened and their father stepped out.

Agnes flew to him and threw her arms around his neck. "Father," she cried. Margaret was close on her heels and they were soon embracing in a three-way hug.

"My children," Father whispered, "I never thought to see you here." He glanced around. "But you are in danger. Please. You must go back where you came from. It's not safe for you here."

"How is Mother? Is she well?" Agnes asked.

"Aye," Father said, "but she misses all of you. We both do." He disengaged himself from them. "Now, go. Before it's too late!" The girls kissed him and turned back toward the edge of the village where Thomas waited. Margaret was eager to tell him they'd seen Father.

Before they had gone far, she heard footfalls behind them. Her stomach knotted itself into a hard ball as she glanced over her shoulder. *Jesus, protect us.* The stranger who had questioned them in front of the tolbooth was following them. "Stop, lassies," he commanded. Knowing they could never outrun him, they obeyed.

29

THIEVES' HOLE

Panic gripped Margaret as the stranger spoke. "My name is Patrick Stewart."

Why had he followed them? He sounded much friendlier than he had back at the tolbooth. But he looked at them with the steely eyes of a lawyer cross-examining a witness. She didn't trust him.

"I saw you talking with your father," he said. "You look cold. And hungry. Come home with me and warm yourself by our fire. Mrs. Stewart will prepare you something to eat."

His smooth-tongued manner did nothing to ease Margaret's tension.

"Mr. Wilson and I have done business together in the past," Patrick said. "He would be welcome to come, too—if he is still in Wigtown."

If he really is Father's friend, it would be rude to refuse. They each carried one of Widow M'Lauchlan's thick bannocks, but they had been too occupied watching for Father to think about eating. By now Agnes must be hungry as well as frightened. Margaret shot another prayer heavenward and then said, "Thank you. We would appreciate that."

Mr. Stewart led the girls to his home and seated them beside the hearth. Margaret relaxed in front of the glowing peat fire, grateful for the warmth of the room. She was tired, and the peat reek, comforting. She fought to keep her eyes open as their host blethered on and on. Minutes passed. She discreetly sniffed the air anticipating the aroma of something warm. There was none. She strained her ears hoping to hear movement in the kitchen. Silence. Patrick excused himself and left the room. At last he must be asking his wife to bring the food he promised. A bowl of steaming broth would be most welcome.

Instead of food, Patrick returned with some wine. "A toast!" he announced. Both girls stared at him in unbelief. "A toast to the king!"

Margaret felt the color draining from her face. "No, thank you!"

"What? You lassies refuse a toast to our new king?"

Agnes began to cry, and Margaret's anger at his deception overpowered her fear. "We must go." She rose from her chair with Agnes clinging to her arm.

Patrick Stewart bolted from the room and shouted, "They're in here!"

Half a dozen soldiers charged in. One clapped his hand on Margaret's shoulder while the other grabbed the sobbing Agnes by the arm.

"Well done, Patrick!" one of them said. "You'll get your reward as soon as we deliver these trophies to the tolbooth!"

Margaret and Agnes exchanged terrified glances as the soldiers dragged them from the house and marched them back the way they had come. When they reached the tolbooth, they were pushed inside with Patrick Stewart trailing behind them.

"Look who Patrick found," one of the troopers gloated. "We've been on the lookout for these rebels for weeks." He turned to the girls' betrayer and smirked. "It's too bad you only found two of them, Patrick. You must go back and find the third one."

The magistrate reached into his desk and hauled out his money bag. He counted out the reward money to Patrick and dismissed him. Turning to the troopers, he said, "There's no room for them here, but there's plenty across the way in Thieves' Hole. Take them away!"

Thieves' Hole! God help us, Margaret prayed silently.

The troopers seized the girls and marched them across High Street to the coal cellar. They dragged them to the entrance of the dark pit and waited while one of the soldiers removed the heavy iron covering that would shut them in. Without the tiniest shred of pity, the troopers shoved the terrified girls into the inky darkness.

Clank! The lid closed over their heads. The cell was so dark, they dared not let go of each other. Agnes began to weep. "Meggie, I'm so scared. I think I'm going to puke."

Margaret could scarcely hear her sister's words above the roar of the blood pounding in her ears. The terrors of the unknown frightened her as much as the darkness. The air was foul. The cellar was cold. She was fearful that they were not alone. She listened for the sound of breathing. *Dear God, protect us. We don't know who or what is in this place.* "God is with us here in the dark, Aggie. He's watching over us, and we're safe in his hands." She hoped her words would encourage her sister. She needed to hear them herself. "When we're afraid, we can trust Jesus to take care of us." But even as she spoke, she felt Agnes go limp in her arms.

Cradling her sister close, Margaret eased herself down to the cold ground. "Aggie," she said tenderly but firmly, "Aggie, wake up." After shaking her sister several times, Margaret decided that Agnes hadn't really fainted. Overcome by shock and fatigue, she had fallen into an exhausted sleep.

If only I had listened to Thomas. Then we would be safe back in the farmhouse. She swallowed to keep her sobs at bay. *Dear God, what have I done? It's all my fault. Father, forgive me.* She could hold back her tears no longer. But, mercifully, she fell asleep, still holding Agnes in her weary arms.

"Meggie, Meggie, wake up."

Margaret's eyes flew open. The darkness reminded her where she was.

"What is it, Agnes?" Margaret whispered.

"There's somebody outside. I hear footsteps."

The footsteps grew louder. "Let's back away from the opening," Margaret said, trying to sound calm, despite the racket her heart was making.

Quietly the iron lid was moved away from the mouth of Thieves' Hole, allowing a shaft of light from the setting sun to pierce the darkness. The girls crouched low and listened as someone cautiously descended the stairs. Whoever it was appeared to be alone. When the figure reached the bottom step, Margaret could see it was a man. In one hand he carried a burning peat, and in the other, a basket. Terror gripped her like a vice as the stranger raised the peat over his head. *Dear God, protect us.*

30

A Welcome Guest

"Don't be afraid," the stranger said. He held the burning peat high as he searched the shadowy cell for the two prisoners. He took a few slow steps toward them. "I have brought you some supper." He held out the basket. "My name is William Moir. I am clerk of the burgh. I see your father each week at the magistrate's office." He paused as if to give the girls time to get over their fright. "I will help you any way I can."

Can this man be trusted? Or is he another Judas, like Patrick Stewart? Margaret hesitated to accept the basket. Why had he come? Had the Lord sent him in answer to her prayers? How could things get any worse?

Margaret's common sense overcame her misgivings. "Thank you," she said extending her right arm while hanging on to Agnes with the other. Once she had the basket in her hand, she was surprised at how heavy it was.

"I know you're terrified to be hidden away in the darkness," Mr. Moir said. "I will leave the peat so you can look around." He smiled. "Now I must go." He handed the burning peat to Agnes. "I'll come again when I can." He turned and disappeared up the steps.

The girls stood motionless until they heard him slide the iron cover over the opening. Silence returned to their cell, but their darkness was pierced by the light of the burning peat. Even a little light was a blessing, though they knew it wouldn't burn for long. Still, it gave a bit of warmth and cheer. Margaret took the peat and raised it as high as she could for a look around the coal cellar. It appeared to be about as large as the main room of their house in Glenvernoch. *Too bad it doesn't have a well-stocked larder. Or a bed. Or at least a place to sit.* But there was nothing in Thieves' Hole to make them comfortable.

"Before the peat burns out, let's see what is in the basket," she said. The girls sat down on the cold ground and removed the cloth. Agnes reached inside and drew out an oatcake. Margaret found another. Under the oatcakes was a skin of buttermilk. Reaching deeper into the basket, she touched a long waxy stick. "Look, Agnes. God is good to us." She lifted out a thick candle.

Agnes reached into the basket again. "There are three more in there," she said in a voice filled with gratitude.

Margaret looked at the peat that was gradually burning up. "Let's light one candle before the peat burns out," she said.

Agnes held one of them up to the peat until it caught fire. With the additional light, the girls returned their precious food to the basket except for two oatcakes, which they ate in silence.

As Margaret enjoyed the fresh oatcake, she thought of the bannocks they had brought with them that morning. She searched for hers in the folds of her skirt. Aye, it was still there, though a bit crumbled. "Do you still have your bannock from Widow M'Lauchlan?"

Agnes checked the folds in her skirt. "Aye," she said drawing it out. She unwrapped it by the light of the candle. "It looks almost as good as when you brought it home."

"Mr. Moir knew we wouldn't get any supper," Margaret said.

"I am going to pray for breakfast and another burning peat," Agnes said.

"I will pray for the same thing. We can keep our bannocks a little longer."

"I wonder if Thomas ate his while he waited for us," Agnes said. "What do you think he did when we didn't come back?"

Margaret had been wondering the same thing. "I don't know." She hoped he hadn't come looking for them and ended up getting caught. "When he wasn't praying for us, I suppose he tramped about humming the psalms."

"Do you think he knows what happened to us?"

Margaret shrugged. "Perhaps." Sensing Agnes's fear for his safety, she added, "He probably waited until the sun began to set before going into the village to look for us. He would take care not to be seen." She gently squeezed Agnes's thin shoulder. "If he knows we've been caught by the dragoons, he will find a way to help us."

"Lady Stewart warned us life would be hard as fugitives," Agnes said, sniffling into her sleeve. Margaret drew her closer as the peat slowly burned itself out.

"Aye," Margaret said, "and so did Widow M'Lauchlan." She watched the peat until all that was left was a single glowing coal. "I wonder how things are with her. And with Lady Stewart." Silently she thanked the Lord for bringing these two Covenant women into their lives.

"I'd like to see them both again," Agnes said. "I hope they are not in as much trouble as we are."

"Let's pray for them," Margaret said.

"I'm so glad we saw Father," Agnes said, "but I really want to see Mother. Do you think we will ever see her again?"

"We'll ask the Lord to make that happen," Margaret said. "Let's sit on my cloak. We can use yours for a blanket. Since it must be night by now, we'll go to sleep with the candle still burning after we pray. Then it won't be so scary."

The girls made their bed as best they could. They knelt to pray, then curled up together and eventually drifted off to a troubled sleep in the cold cellar.

Margaret had no way of knowing when morning came. Both girls were awake when someone removed the iron lid from the entrance to Thieves' Hole. They bolted upright and clutched each other.

A shaft of light pierced the darkness over the steps as three men descended. The first one carried a burning peat, which he gave to Margaret. A second one handed Agnes two spoons and a wooden bowl containing warm porridge. The third had brought a basin and a pitcher of water. As they left the coal cellar, one muttered, "'Tis more than they deserve." The iron lid clanked overhead, shutting out the daylight again.

"Look, Aggie. This peat torch is much longer than the one William Moir brought us. Now we'll have a bit of light for a little while longer—and we can see to wash our hands!"

"I'm thankful for something warm to eat," Agnes said, holding the bowl close to her body. "And for a burning peat to see what it is we're eating."

31

MORE VISITORS

"Listen," Margaret whispered, "it sounds like someone is coming." The iron plate covering the abandoned coal cellar was again drawn back. Clutching each other, the girls shrank away from the stairs. Margaret peered toward the opening, trying to see who was entering. A man with a candle in his right hand limped down the steps. He paused as if waiting for his eyes to adjust to the darkness. Heart pounding, Margaret held her breath and stared at him. And then she rushed forward. "Father! Oh, Father! How did you know we were here?"

Mr. Wilson enveloped his daughters in a hug. When at last he found his voice, he said. "Thomas told me."

"How did he know?" Margaret asked.

"When you didn't return to him, he went looking for you." Mr. Wilson wiped his eyes with the back of his hand. "He saw you being taken to the tolbooth. And then to this place. He hurried home to tell me." He paused for breath. "I feared for your safety after I saw you at the tolbooth." His sad voice was tainted with anger. Or was it bitterness? "I prayed you would be kept safe, but . . . God has stopped answering my prayers."

He sighed softly and then asked, "Tell me what happened after I saw you, lassies."

Margaret explained how Patrick Stewart had tricked them. "He's the devil in disguise," she said. "He pretended to be your friend and offered us food and warmth so he could betray us!" Her shoulders shook with fury. "Then the wretch collected his coins for turning us in. May the Lord repay him for his treachery!"

"I have but fifteen minutes," Father said. He handed Agnes a large basket. "Mother has sent you food and blankets. You'll find half a dozen candles inside the blankets."

"Oooooh, thank you," Margaret said when she saw the bannocks and oatcakes. "And buttermilk, too!"

A shadow appeared at the opening. "I must go," Father said. He hugged his daughters once more.

"Tell Mother we love her," Agnes said, as tears streamed from her eyes.

"Monday morning I'll set out for Edinburgh. I'll plead your case before the Privy Council," he promised. "I won't stop until I secure your release." He handed his candle to Agnes, turned, and limped up the stairs. Margaret followed him with her eyes until the iron plate shut out the daylight. She heard him speak briefly with someone outside. She did not move until the hoof beats of his horse faded away.

Silence enveloped the girls as they clung to each other and sobbed themselves to sleep. Meanwhile, Father's candle burned itself out.

After they awakened, the girls sat for hours talking about Mother and Father and the comfortable home they had left behind. Margaret's thoughts fled to Fergus in Drumjargon, but she kept them to herself. They relived their days of sleeping in the cave and worshiping in the outdoors with the hill people. They talked about Thomas. "I wish he were here," Agnes said. "I miss him."

"Aye." Margaret prayed he was safe back at the farmhouse.

When they ran out of things to talk about, they sat in silence. Time passed slowly, and Margaret fretted because she had no way of knowing if it were day or night. Eventually she fell asleep again. She awakened to the sound of the iron cover being moved.

Two soldiers brought them food and a burning peat. They departed without a word.

"The Lord has not forgotten us," Margaret said as they ate their breakfast, "and we must not forget him." She took another bite of her stale oatcake. "Since it's daylight outside, it must be the Lord's Day." She sighed. "I suppose my Mr. Colquhoun is still ranting against us Covenanters."

"He made us sound like wicked lawbreakers, didn't he?" Agnes said.

Margaret nodded. "He would be happy to know where we are right now." Dismissing the infuriating minister from her mind, Margaret said, "We will have our own worship service right here. We can sing our favorite psalms, just as we did at kirk. But we won't have to listen to a boring rant by Mr. Colquhoun." She lit a candle from the flickering peat. Then she patted the deep pocket of her skirt in search of the verses Fergus had copied for her. She pulled them out and tried to read them. "One candle doesn't give enough light to see the tiny writing," she said, "but we can talk about the Scriptures we've memorized."

And so the two worshiped the Lord by flickering candlelight. When the light burned out, they again talked about the things they missed most: home and friends. "I wonder what it will be like to live with Jesus in heaven," Agnes said.

"I don't know exactly what heaven is like," Margaret said. "But I am sure it will be a wonderful place because Jesus is there." Eventually the girls drifted off to sleep, huddled together to keep warm.

A loud scraping awakened Margaret. The iron lid was lifted away from the mouth of Thieves' Hole. Sunlight flooded the stairs, and harsh voices filled the dark recesses of the coal cellar. Margaret cowered beside Agnes in the corner opposite the steps. Too frightened to move, she watched as an old woman was shoved down the stairs. "You can pray as long as you wish down there," a hard voice barked.

The new prisoner cried out as the iron lid clanged shut over her head. And then there was silence.

Margaret sat motionless, wondering what to do. The woman must be as frightened as they were when they were thrust into Thieves' Hole. *How can I let her know we're here without startling her?* Margaret's compassion overcame her hesitation, and she called out, "Hello."

The newcomer gasped. More silence. "You are not alone," Margaret said. "My sister and I are prisoners, too."

Then the new woman spoke. Her voice sounded old but not defeated. "May Jesus Christ be praised," she said. "Is your name Margaret?"

"Aye, but how did you know that?"

The stranger laughed softly. "I am Widow M'Lauchlan," she said.

"Widow M'Lauchlan! Hold your hands out in front of you and keep talking. We'll find you." And with that the two sisters, holding tight to each other, edged toward the voice that called to them.

"There you are!" Margaret whispered as her fingers touched the thin fingers of the precious saint who had taught them so much about the Covenanters.

"We've thought of you often," Margaret said. "We wished we could see you again. This isn't what we had in mind."

Widow M'Lauchlan chuckled as she embraced them. "That's all right," she said. "I've been expecting a visit from the dragoons, so I made a few plans myself. I've brought half a dozen candles with me." Margaret heard the smile in her voice. "We will ask the Lord to send us a light. When he does, these candles will brighten this dreary old Thieves' Hole." As she spoke, she sniffed the air. "I smell peat reek!"

"Aye, you do," Agnes said. "Twice the Lord has sent us a burning peat. I'm sure he'll answer your prayer for a light."

"Mr. Moir from the tolbooth brought us food and a burning peat the first night we were here," Margaret added. "We found candles in the bottom of his food basket. Then Father brought us six more. This morning the soldiers brought a burning peat along with our breakfast. We lit one of our candles each morning before the peat burned out."

"We've burned two candles," Agnes said. "We don't want to use them up too fast."

"God ne'er sent the mouth, but he sent the meat wi't," Widow M'Lauchlan said. "He will give us what we need, including a light for our candles here in the darkness. We should thank him for that. Then we can talk."

Widow M'Lauchlan's words encouraged Margaret. But it would take more than reassuring words to get them out of the dank old Thieves' Hole. She must pray for a miracle.

32

MUSINGS IN THIEVES' HOLE

"How long have you been in this dreadful place?" Widow M'Lauchlan asked.

"Not long," Margaret replied. "We were tossed down here like a pair of worn-out boots two days ago."

"I thank the Lord for bringing me to you."

"We thank him, too," Margaret said. "The Lord couldn't have chosen a more encouraging 'angel' to help us in our trials."

"We can encourage one another," the widow said. "A three-strand cord cannot be easily broken. Let's praise God for his goodness and seek him for his strength."

When the prayer ended, worry crept back into Margaret's mind. "It's so dark in this place, we can't tell day from night. Or when one day ends and another begins," she said. "It seems like we've been here two weeks!"

"I suppose it does," Widow M'Lauchlan said softly. "Now that the Lord has brought us together, the time will pass much faster." She chuckled. "We have lots of time to sing and pray together without being interrupted."

Agnes shivered as she clung to Margaret. "Meggie," she whispered, "can we sit down?"

"Of course," said Margaret, searching with her right foot for the blankets Father had brought them. "We'll sit on one of the blankets and cover ourselves with the others. We can squeeze together to keep warm." When she found their blankets, she patted one flat with her hands. "There," she said, reaching out to Agnes and Widow M'Lauchlan. "This should keep out some of the cold."

The women tucked Agnes between them and pulled the other blankets over themselves. For the first time since they were thrust into Thieves' Hole, Margaret felt warm. How good it was to have someone older and wiser to share their troubles! Before long, all three were fast asleep.

Margaret awakened with her leg numb from sitting with Agnes slumped against her. As she stirred, the others woke up. "I'm sorry," she said trying to get comfortable.

"No need to apologize," Widow M'Lauchlan assured her. "We'll have lots of time for sleep."

"I'm surprised that the dragoons were able to catch you," Margaret said. "You've been so clever in avoiding them."

"Well," said the widow, "there has been a rumor around the village that you girls and your brother were hiding out near Wigtown. When you showed up at my cottage, I surmised that you were living in the abandoned farmhouse deep in the hollow. I was happy to see you, but I feared you might have been seen." She cleared her throat. "We don't get many visitors in winter. When an outsider comes, he's questioned along with anyone he visits."

Margaret scowled in the darkness. *Am I responsible for Widow M'Lauchlan's imprisonment, too?* She sighed. *God forgive me for being so foolhardy!*

"After you left me, I asked the Lord to take you safely back to your hidey hole," Widow M'Lauchlan said. She hesitated before adding, "As I prayed for you, I told the Lord I would like to see you again."

Both girls gasped. "But not in Thieves' Hole," Margaret said.

"No, but not to worry," Widow M'Lauchlan said. "The Lord has a plan for each of us. When we walk with him, we do not walk alone." Margaret could hear a smile in her voice as she added, "Our lives are God's gift to us. He alone determines when they are to be taken away."

"I'm glad he is mightier than those vicious dragoons sent out to look for us," Margaret said. "If it weren't for the Lord's protection, we could have been captured more than once."

"I stayed on my knees most of last night praying for you—and for all the hill folk. This morning my prayers were interrupted by pounding at my door. Before I could rise to answer, two rough soldiers stormed into my cottage. They wagged a paper in my face."

The muscles in Margaret's throat tightened. She could almost see the words on that paper.

"One of the soldiers snarled at me, demanding that I go with them." She sighed. "How could I resist?" She laughed quietly. "I made them wait while I gathered a few things I wanted to take along."

Margaret tried to hold back her tears, but she couldn't. "It's my fault," she sobbed, "my fault the soldiers took you away, isn't it?"

Widow M'Lauchlan put a comforting arm around her. "Not necessarily," she said. "Remember, Margaret, it is the Lord who directs our paths." She paused and added, "Maybe your coming to see me was part of his plan for bringing us together."

Margaret felt so confused. *God's plan or my stupidity?*

Widow M'Lauchlan sighed. "For years my husband and I defied those ruffians foisted on us by King Charles. We refused to attend the services in Kirkinner parish. After my husband died, I continued to help the Covenanters whenever I could."

"I wish I could be just like you," Margaret said. "You don't complain about what happens to you. You just keep on trusting the Lord to watch over you." She was eager to hear the rest of her friend's story. "What happened after the soldiers took you away?"

"At the tolbooth, one of Claverhouse's dragoons shoved a paper into my face. It was a list of people from our parish who had not been showing up for the services each Lord's Day."

"But if you haven't attended kirk for years, why did the minister report you now?" Margaret asked.

"Only a handful of people attend Kirkinner kirk these days. They've told me that Mr. Symson speaks mostly to the rafters. Unlike many ministers today, he's a well-educated man. I suppose it hurts his pride that scarcely anyone attends kirk anymore in his parish. At any rate, he reported me." She chuckled. "My name headed the list of disorderly parishioners who don't attend the services."

The sound of the lid to Thieves' Hole interrupted their conversation. The captives blinked when daylight hit their eyes. A rough-looking man descended and shoved a tin plate into Widow M'Lauchlan's hands. By the light of the peat torch they saw three wizened oatcakes and a skin of buttermilk. Then he handed Margaret his burning peat and disappeared as quickly as he had come.

"The Lord has provided," Widow M'Lauchlan said, and there was no trace of surprise in her voice.

"Well," said Margaret as she chewed and chewed, "this food will certainly last us for a long time. I wonder when we'll get another fine meal."

As she jested, she remembered the thick bannocks she had brought home from Widow M'Lauchlan's house a week ago. She and Agnes had agreed to save them as long as they could. She searched until she found hers in her skirt, now considerably flattened.

"Agnes and I have something to share with you," she said.

"We do?" Agnes asked.

"Remember what we brought along to eat when we came to see Father?"

"Aye," said Agnes. She searched her clothing and pulled hers out. "Widow M'Lauchlan," she said, "hold out your hand."

"Whatever are you giving to me?"

Now both girls were giggling. "It's one of the fat bannocks you sent home with Margaret!" said Agnes. "She has one, also."

"Well, well, well," Widow M'Lauchlan said. "Week-old bannocks are better than no bread. Now we'll have something for supper if our jailers forget us."

"How long do you think they will keep us here?" Margaret asked.

"Only the Lord knows," Widow M'Lauchlan replied. "Until he delivers us from our enemies, we can spend our time remembering his promises and thanking him for his presence." She lowered her voice and said, "I wouldn't mind being here so much if I could see to read the Scriptures." Then she sighed. "They could have given us a little lantern and a bed." She stretched her arms and legs. "I could use a little heat, too "

"So could we," said Agnes, as the three of them squeezed closer to one another.

"We must keep trusting the Lord," said Widow M'Lauchlan. "It will be easier to do that together."

"I want to ask him to protect Thomas," Agnes said.

"I'll ask him to watch over Father and Mother," Margaret added. *What will happen now that Father has openly acknowledged us? Will the authorities punish him even more severely?*

33

TO MACHERMORE CASTLE DUNGEON

Time moved a little faster during the next few days. The prisoners enjoyed a bit of light each morning when breakfast and another burning peat were brought to their cell, along with a pitcher of water. When the iron plate shut them in once more, they huddled around the lighted peat until it was nearly burned out. Then they lit one of their precious candles.

Widow M'Lauchlan never tired of answering their questions about the Covenanters. Agnes cringed when she related the sufferings of Hugh M'Kail, who refused to renounce his faith even when tortured by the boot.

"Before he was hanged, he lifted the napkin from his face and said the angels in heaven were preparing to carry his soul to God," she said.

Margaret vowed in her heart she'd never give up her faith in Christ. *Please, God, keep me walking with you no matter what happens to me.*

One day Widow M'Lauchlan told them about two harsh laws that were being enforced against the Covenanters. "Last

November," she began, "the government passed the Bloody Act. That was a good name for it, too, because the murders of innocent Covenanters have increased ever since."

"Bloody Act?" Margaret said. She wasn't sure she wanted to know more. Yet she was curious.

"It's a make-over of the Test Act, but it's worse. Anyone suspected of being disloyal must swear loyalty to the king on the spot." Widow M'Lauchlan sighed deeply as if her spirit ached. "Taking the oath shows you support the king—that you agree that the kirk should be run by the state. But here's the worst part. All Covenanters are now forced to swear the Abjuration Oath denouncing James Renwick!" She spat out the words as though they tasted bitter on her tongue.

"Never! No one can force us to do either!" Margaret sputtered.

"Aye, 'tis a sad state," Widow M'Lauchlan said. "Every man, woman, and child of fourteen years and over is forced to kneel and swear the Test *with* the Abjuration Oath."

"And if we don't?" Margaret asked, growing more upset by the minute.

Widow M'Lauchlan paused a long while before continuing. "Those who refuse are executed on the spot."

"God help us!" Margaret cried. Suddenly, being locked up in the coal cellar didn't seem so bad. "What about the families of those who are executed? Are they punished?"

"Aye," Widow M'Lauchlan said. "Children twelve and up are sometimes held responsible for other family members, along with their parents. Some men are imprisoned. Others are sent to dungeons. Or to plantations in the West Indies or America."

The sobering news left Margaret speechless.

"Enough of that kind of talk," Widow M'Lauchlan said. "We must think of more pleasant things. Like the love Jesus Christ has for us and the assurance that we will one day be with him forever."

For the rest of the day, she taught the girls the Scriptures. She reminded them of the ones they had already learned and related new truths, which Margaret absorbed with eagerness. And she never tired of encouraging them to keep trusting the Lord. One day, after she had been with them for a week, she said, "Let's sing, like Paul and Silas did when they were in prison."

"I would like that," Agnes said.

For the next hour or so they sang as many of the psalms as they could remember. When the girls' memories failed them, Widow M'Lauchlan supplied the missing words. The joyful praises lifted Margaret's spirits, and the sounds drifted up from the coal cellar to the street above. Encouraged by the words they sang, they huddled together and fell asleep.

They were awakened several hours later by the sound of the cover being slid from Thieves' Hole. Whoever was coming was very quiet and carried nothing to light his way down the steps.

"Don't be afraid. I am your brother in Christ," William Moir said in a loud whisper. "I have news for you." He scanned the cellar in the faint light of dusk that filtered down from the opening. "People heading to the magistrate's office have been listening to your singing. Provost Coltrane is upset. He has ordered Widow M'Lauchlan to be taken to Machermore Castle dungeon tomorrow. She will be held there until she is brought to trial."

"Please, God, no!" Margaret cried out and Agnes burst into tears.

Mr. Moir reached into his jacket and pulled out a sack of candles and three bannocks. He handed them to Widow M'Lauchlan. "I'm sorry I could not risk lighting a peat and bringing it to you."

"Thank you for your kindness," Widow M'Lauchlan said.

"I'll be praying for you," said Mr. Moir. He turned and left as quietly as he had come.

Once he was gone, the sisters clung to the widow, overcome with grief and fear.

"Hush now, my dears," she said gently. "I'll be leaving you, but the Lord Jesus will still be with you here—and with me at Machermore Castle. My husband used to say, 'He that would eat the fruit must climb the tree.' I am willing to suffer whatever I must, to hear the Lord say, 'Well done, good and faithful servant.' "

Margaret tried to control her thoughts. "We will miss you so much. Thank you for all the things you've taught us."

"I will miss you, too," Widow M'Lauchlan said. "And I will pray for you often." Her voice was full of determination. "Now don't you worry about me. I want to share one more story. To help you face whatever lies ahead. Let me tell it, and then we need to sleep."

The three women dropped down on their blankets. "In the book of Numbers, God tells us about the offerings at the dedication of the tabernacle," the widow said. "The heads of families brought oxen for the leaders of the twelve tribes. Some of the oxen would help in their work. The others would be sacrificed as they worshiped the Lord. So, you see, some oxen were given for service. Others were given for sacrifice.

"The Lord gives us many opportunities to serve him," she continued. "Just like those oxen given to the leaders, we have work to do for him. But," she added, "a time may come when service is not what the Lord asks of us. Instead he may ask for sacrifice. When that happens, we need to be just as willing to give what he asks."

She paused, allowing the sisters time to think about what she had just told them. "Don't worry about me," she said. "But do pray for me. Pray that I will have light enough to read the Scriptures I have with me. And pray it won't be long until we are brought to trial."

Margaret struggled to hold in her sobs, and she felt Agnes raise her cloak to wipe away her own tears.

"I would enjoy returning to my home in Drumjargon, if God so wills it," the widow said. "But he knows that I am ready for service. Or for sacrifice." On the last word, Widow M'Lauchlan's voice choked with emotion. It was some time before she could continue.

Margaret thought about her own life in the light of what her friend had said. *Service or sacrifice? Service or sacrifice?* She fell asleep with those two words jousting in her mind.

Next morning, shortly after the prisoners had received breakfast and a lighted peat, two surly troopers descended into Thieves' Hole. "We've come for Widow M'Lauchlan," one of them growled.

The precious Covenanter hugged each girl to her heart and whispered in her ear. Then, she stepped forward and, without complaining, followed the troopers up the steps and into the light.

Margaret watched her go, head high and footsteps firm. Too overcome with grief to speak, she and Agnes sank onto their blankets in silence. If it pleased the Lord, soon they would be brought to trial, along with Widow M'Lauchlan. *For service? Or for sacrifice? What will the verdict be?*

34

TRIAL AND SENTENCING

Margaret and Agnes shielded their eyes as they stepped into the bright sunshine. After three weeks in the inky darkness of the old coal cellar, the sunlight caused them pain. They stumbled along between the armed soldiers who led them to the courtroom. They were marched to a row of wooden chairs, where a thin and unkempt man and a woman stared at them through hopeless eyes. "Sit here," one of the soldiers ordered, pointing to a couple of empty seats in the row. They took their places, facing the magistrate's desk.

Soon Widow M'Lauchlan was escorted into the courtroom by two ruffians. One look at their gaunt, disheveled friend and Margaret knew she had suffered much in Machermore dungeon. *How sad that dear old saint cannot go down to her grave in peace.*

The three friends were allowed to greet each other. Then Widow M'Lauchlan sat down beside Margaret. "The other Covenanters on trial today," she whispered, nodding her head toward the man and woman who shared the prisoners' row, "are Margaret Maxwell of Barquhannie and William Kerr of Boreland."

At that moment, the four tyrants who would decide their fate filed into the room and took their places. One was Sir Robert Grierson of Lagg, now knighted for his efforts to wipe out the Covenanters. A bloodthirsty persecutor who killed for pleasure. By comparison, his savagery made Claverhouse appear sensitive.

Widow M'Lauchlan leaned close to Margaret again and whispered in her ear to identify the other judges. "David Graham is Claverhouse's brother. Captain Strachan and Major Winram are dragoon leaders in Wigtown," she explained. "We can expect no mercy from any of them."

Margaret breathed deeply to calm her racing heart, but it didn't help much. *Be merciful to us, O God.*

"Stand to hear the charges against you," Grierson commanded.

The captives stood, and he began to read the indictments. "You are hereby charged with rebellion at Bothwell Bridge and at Airds Moss."

Margaret gritted her teeth at the false accusations. "Your honor, we have never been to those places," she protested. "When those battles were fought, I was twelve years old and Agnes was only six."

Grierson ignored her and thundered out the second charge. "You are furthermore charged with having attended twenty field conventicles."

Again Margaret spoke up. "We worship with the hill folk, rather than listening to the preaching of hirelings at kirk." Knowing the outcome of the trial had already been decided, her anger was fast overcoming her fears. Once she began defending herself, she felt a Power from above leading her on. "We would have attended twenty conventicles if we could have done so."

Grierson's face reddened at Margaret's boldness. "There is one final charge. You have refused to swear the Abjuration Oath!"

Staring Grierson full in the face, she stated, "I have *not* refused to swear the Abjuration Oath. It was never offered to me."

"Well, then," Grierson bellowed to an officer in the court, "give it to her right now."

Margaret stared at Grierson with unflinching determination. "I condemn the unjust slaughter of those of us who differ in our faith just as Reverend Renwick did in his declaration. I will *never* denounce him or his teachings!"

She gulped and then went on, not giving Grierson opportunity to interrupt her. "The persecution against us Covenanters forces us to defend our beliefs. Beliefs which you should know are based on what the Scriptures teach." She aimed one last look at Grierson before adding, "I was not present to sign Reverend Renwick's declaration. But if I had been, I would have signed it!"

Grierson grimaced. "She speaks only for herself," he said with venom. "Give the oath to the others." But when the officer tried, they too refused to take it.

"You all deserve to die!" Grierson shouted. Throwing legal procedure to the winds, the court delivered the sentences immediately. "I order you to your knees to receive your sentences," he barked.

Emboldened through her silent prayers, Margaret refused to kneel. So did Widow M'Lauchlan and Agnes. In a flash, the soldiers forced them to their knees and held them down while the sentences were pronounced.

"Margaret Wilson, Agnes Wilson, and Widow M'Lauchlan! Upon the eleventh of May you shall be tied to stakes fixed within the flood mark in the water of Bladnoch, near Wigtown where the sea flows at high water. There you will stand 'til the flood overflows you and drowns you!"

We're to be drowned? Margaret raised her eyes to Grierson. One glance at his smug expression, and she understood. He intended to make their execution a forceful display of his power.

A look of quiet acceptance passed between her and Widow M'Lauchlan. An anguished cry burst from Agnes's throat. Margaret pulled her close as she sobbed loudly. "Don't give up, Aggie," she whispered in her ear. "God is with us, and he's still in charge." She continued to hold her.

"Margaret Maxwell, kneel to receive your sentence." As she knelt before him, he continued, "You are hereby sentenced to be flogged through the streets of Wigtown on three successive days. Subsequent to each flogging, you will be chained in the town jougs at the tolbooth for an hour.

Margaret Maxwell began to weep with relief.

Why, Margaret Wilson wondered, *has she received a lighter sentence than the rest of us? Is it because she has been quieter about her beliefs? Or is it because the Lord has chosen her for service?*

She shuddered when William Kerr was banished to the colonies in America. Who would care for his family?

Following the sentencing, the five prisoners were taken to cells in the tolbooth. The sisters were separated from Widow M'Lauchlan. Margaret looked around at their new quarters. Whatever the conditions here, they would be an improvement over Thieves' Hole. She thanked the Lord when she caught sight of a small window on one wall of the cell.

A few days later Margaret noticed additional guards had come on duty. Listening to a conversation that came in her window from the street, she learned that William Kerr had escaped. She stared at the four walls that would keep her and Agnes confined until the day of their execution. *Lord, I am ready to sacrifice my life in honor of Jesus, true head of the kirk,* she prayed silently. *But please deliver Agnes. Just as you delivered Daniel from the hungry lions, you can deliver Agnes from these murderers.*

35

REPRIEVE

The Wilson sisters huddled together on their blankets in their basement cell in the tolbooth. Margaret thanked the Lord for the little window just above eye level. Light filtered in between the bars, and overhearing the conversation of people passing by helped her feel less isolated. She studied her frail sister, leaning hard on her shoulder. *She's much braver than I expected*, Margaret thought. But Agnes had grown more fragile during their weeks of confinement in Thieves' Hole. Margaret wanted to encourage her. But what could she say to a thirteen-year-old facing execution within a month?

Margaret had prayed every day for her father's efforts to get them released. Remembering the determination in his eyes when he had visited them in Thieves' Hole, she knew he wouldn't give up working for their freedom, and she wouldn't give up praying. But even as she prayed, doubts troubled her mind.

Her thoughts scattered at the sound of voices and footsteps outside the prison cell. One voice was loud and belligerent; the other, much softer. She strained to hear what they were saying. "I have ridden four days to Edinburgh to secure my daughter's release. A bond of one hundred pounds! That's how I purchased her freedom. You *must* let me take her home!"

It was Father's voice. Margaret hugged Agnes. The voices were near the door now. Her heart pounded at the sound of the bolt being removed. The door swung open. "Father!" the girls cried, rushing into his arms.

"I've come to take you home," he said to Agnes.

Provost Coltrane allowed them only a few minutes together. "Come!" he said. "I have more important things to do." He strutted toward the door.

Father held Margaret close in a farewell embrace and whispered, "Next week I will return to Edinburgh and beseech the Privy Council to release you and Widow M'Lauchlan from your sentences."

Margaret pulled Agnes close. "You're a brave girl, Aggie," she whispered to her. "Don't worry about me."

Father and Margaret exchanged a look of love and anguish before he took Agnes's hand and followed Provost Coltrane out of the cell. The door slammed shut. Margaret stared at it for a long time after the bolt slid into its place shutting her in.

Margaret's lonely days in her prison cell were interrupted only by someone bringing her food and water. It was hard to keep track of the days, for each one seemed endless. As she waited alone for execution, she passed the time singing and praying and thinking about heaven. She reviewed in her mind the Bible truths Widow M'Lauchlan had taught her during the two weeks they had been together in Thieves' Hole. One story kept running through her mind. The story of the oxen. *For service or for sacrifice?* She had lived in service to the Lord to the best of her ability. Now if he was asking her to lay down her life, she was willing.

Her death would release her from her persecutors and bring her into the Lord's presence. What a joy it would be to see Jesus face to face! Yet she grieved as she thought of leaving her family, especially Agnes. Sweet Agnes. So determined to follow Jesus, even though she was terrified of what lay ahead. *Jesus, may she remember you are always with her and that you'll help her cope regardless of what happens.*

She thought of Thomas, her boon companion, and wondered if he was still hiding out in the old farmhouse. And what had happened to her older brothers who had fled to Ireland some years earlier? She wished she knew what had happened to them after they fled Glenvernoch. She regretted how much Mother and Father had suffered because of their children's convictions. *I know they love us, Lord, even though their faith is not strong enough to stand against the king.*

One evening William Moir brought her supper. She was surprised and pleased because she'd seen no friendly face since Father had taken Agnes home. Mr. Moir handed her food and then walked toward the corner of the cell away from the door. He beckoned her to come closer. When she did, he spoke softly and quickly.

"I have two things to tell you. After your father took Agnes home, he went to Edinburgh to petition the Privy Council on your behalf. I myself sent a letter to the Privy Council on behalf of Widow M'Lauchlan."

A letter on behalf of Widow M'Lauchlan. "What a kind thing for you to do," Margaret said.

He looked embarrassed and added, "I wrote as if I were she. I said I was willing to swear the Abjuration Oath. I entreated the council to show compassion in view of my age," Mr. Moir said. "I also said that the sentence pronounced against me was just."

Stunned at what he had done, Margaret dropped her eyes and prayed some good might come from this dishonest deed.

"I finished the letter with a promise to attend kirk and conform to the king's edicts. I signed it, 'Margaret M'Lauchlan.' Then I secured the signatures of John Dunbar and William Gordon as witnesses, before forwarding it to the Privy Council." He paused uncertainly and then smiled. "I hope that my letter, along with your father's personal request, will secure a pardon for the devout old lady."

Margaret shook her head in despair. Widow M'Lauchlan would never swear the Abjuration Oath. Nor would she compear as His Royal Highness demanded. "Widow M'Lauchlan is ready to die whenever the Lord calls her home," Margaret said. "And so am I. If the eleventh of May is the day he has chosen, we will gladly say good-bye to this world." Her eyes swimming with tears, Margaret added, "Your intentions were good, Mr. Moir, but honesty is a part of the covenant we hold fast."

Mr. Moir's face turned deep red. "Well, whatever you think of me, I have good news from your father. He wanted to tell you himself, but Provost Coltrane refused to let him visit you. He searched me out and asked me to deliver his message."

Margaret raised her eyes to him, not knowing what to expect.

"Four days ago, on the thirtieth day of April, the lords of the Privy Council recommended that their secretaries secure your reprieve—and that of Widow M'Lauchlan."

A thrill of relief shot through Margaret. Not wanting to miss one single word, she leaned into Mr. Moir. "One of the council members promised your father the reprieves would be sent to Wigtown."

Tears of gratitude rolled down Margaret's cheeks. "The documents haven't arrived yet," Mr. Moir said, and Margaret's heart almost stopped beating. "But don't worry. They have a week to get here before the day of execu—" He could not finish his sentence. He wiped his eyes with his sleeve and turned to leave. Margaret reached out and caught his arm.

"Thank you for bringing me the good news," she whispered. "You have been kind to me ever since I was shoved into Thieves' Hole. May I beg one more favor?"

Mr. Moir took her thin hand in his. "Of course. I will do anything within my power."

"Since Father is not permitted to visit me, will you please bring me some writing materials? I want to send a letter to him and Mother."

Mr. Moir nodded and left the cell. Two days later he returned with paper, inkhorn, and quill. "I'll come back this evening to pick up your letter," he said.

Margaret spent the rest of the day carefully composing the letter . . . what might well be her last words to her parents if the pardon did not arrive in time.

I do not feel alone, she wrote, for I am comforted by the Lord's presence. I gladly accept whatever he has for me. I am completely at his disposal. If he chooses that I die on the eleventh of May, I will go directly into the home he has prepared for me. I cannot ask for a better home. If he chooses to stay the execution, I will await what he has for me with eagerness. He has never failed me yet. I know I can trust him.

No matter how many times the Abjuration Oath is offered to me, I will not save my life by swearing something I do not believe. I cannot conform to teachings that are clearly contrary to the Word of God.

I love you, and I grieve for the losses you have endured on my account. I ask for your forgiveness. I will be waiting to welcome you into heaven when the Lord calls you home.

By the time Mr. Moir brought Margaret her breakfast three days later, he had delivered her letter.

36

HOMECOMING

Margaret spent the evening of May 10 praying about the morrow. If the reprieve from the Privy Council was delivered, she would be released for service. If not, she was ready for sacrifice.

"Lord, I know you won't allow me to suffer more than I can bear," she prayed. Sensing his presence with her in the prison cell, she slept well. Upon awakening once in the middle of the night, she prayed again for her family and for Widow M'Lauchlan.

The next morning, the spring bluebells hung their heads under a drab sky. Though lambs gamboled in the pastures and birdsong filled the air, nothing could dispel the gloom that overhung Wigtown. Every mind was gripped by visions of the tide that would rush into the mud flats in the channel, filling the riverbed to its banks . . . a silent, relentless executioner.

The tramping of heavy feet and loud, mocking voices interrupted Margaret's prayers. Apparently the reprieve that Father was promised did not arrive. Or perhaps it had, and Grierson of Lagg had chosen not to acknowledge it. *That's all right, Jesus.* She ran her fingers through her tangled hair and straightened her tattered clothing as best she could. Her cell door was thrown open, and Major Winram and several soldiers stormed into the room. They surrounded her, grabbed her by the arms, and led her up the stairs and out of the tolbooth. There she saw Widow M'Lauchlan standing quietly between two soldiers. As their eyes met, Widow M'Lauchlan mouthed the word "sacrifice," and Margaret nodded. Today they would be together with Jesus.

"Move along," one of the soldiers ordered, pushing Margaret forward.

After four weeks of confinement Margaret eagerly drew in a long breath. Instead of delightful fresh air, the stench of henbane blossoming in all the dunghills gagged her. How could any plant have such a foul odor? Her hands were not free to hold her nose, so she stopped breathing as long as she could. Once they descended the hill to the river, they'd be away from the stench.

At Major Winram's command, the condemned women were led down to the river by a guard of mocking soldiers. A large procession of weeping townspeople followed, praying that the Lord would stop the executions. The bolder ones entreated the soldiers not to carry out the death sentences.

Margaret glimpsed her parents and tried to give them a smile of reassurance. "I am not afraid," she shouted to them.

Then, standing nearer to the bank, she saw Fergus. Their eyes locked, and everything else disappeared for a brief, comforting moment. Fergus folded his hands in prayer and raised his eyes toward heaven. *Thank you, Lord*, Margaret prayed in her heart. She nodded and smiled before one of the soldiers blocked her view.

Major Winram surveyed the low tide. "Drive a stake at the bottom of the channel for the old woman," he said to one of the soldiers. "I want her nearer the tidal waters." He grinned diabolically. "Watching her struggle against the rising waters just might change the stubborn lass's mind! When she sees what is in store for her, she'll be begging to swear the Test!"

Lord, give me strength, Margaret prayed silently as a soldier pounded a stout wooden stake into the soft silt at the bottom of the channel in the river, near to the advancing tide. A second stake was driven near the top of the channel close to where she stood.

She watched as rough hands shoved her precious friend down the channel to the lower stake. *She's weak and frail. Why do they treat her so harshly?* Margaret flinched when one of the soldiers grabbed the widow's hands and slammed them on either side of the stake. She felt the pain as though it were her own palms being bruised against the rough wood. Another soldier wound a rope round and round the widow's hands and wrists, binding her to the stake as though she were a common criminal. Their fiendish task complete, the soldiers retreated to the shore.

Widow M'Lauchlan glanced up at Margaret, standing at the top of the channel guarded by two soldiers. A slight smile creased the corners of her mouth. Then she bowed her head and stood in silence.

Through the years she showed me how to live out my faith. Now she is showing me how to die. Jesus, I thank you for Widow M'Lauchlan. Thank you that her trials will soon be over.

The soldiers had scarcely finished driving the second stake into the sand when the foam-crested billows began rolling up the river channel. Soon the waters were lapping at Widow M'Lauchlan's feet, as though hungering to devour her. Inch by inch they covered the hem of her gown. Then her hips. Her waistline. Through it all she stood firm. Even when the rushing waters reached her neck, her countenance was calm and peaceful.

Take her, Lord, Margaret prayed.

As the rising tide engulfed Widow M'Lauchlan, Grierson of Lagg and his cohorts began to make sport of her. "What do you see now?" he asked Margaret.

"I see Christ in one of his members wrestling here," Margaret answered. She looked directly into Grierson's eyes. "Do you think we are the only sufferers? No. It is Christ in us who suffers. He sends none of us to fight alone!"

Then Margaret closed her eyes and began to sing.

> O why art thou cast down, my soul?
> why in me so dismayed?
> Trust God, for I shall praise him yet,
> his count'nance is mine aid.

When she heard the crowd gasp in horror, Margaret looked up to see the officer who carried the town halberd holding the drowning saint's head under the water with its broad blade. A handful of bubbles rose above the gray hair now floating on the water's surface. When the bubbles disappeared, the officer returned to his post at the top of the channel.

The soldiers guarding Margaret yanked her toward the stake at the higher end of the channel. Amid the cries and prayers of the people gathered on the shore, they bound her to it as they had done with her friend. Then they retreated to watch the show.

As the hissing and seething waters began to envelop her, she quoted from the eighth chapter of Romans in a strong, steady voice:

Who shall separate us from the love of Christ? Shall tribulation, or distress, or persecution, or famine, or nakedness, or peril, or sword? As it is written, for thy sake we are killed all the day long; we are accounted as sheep for the slaughter. Nay, in all these things we are more than conquerors through him that loved us. For I am persuaded, that neither death, nor life, nor angels, nor principalities, nor powers, nor things present, nor things to come, nor height, nor depth, nor any other creature, shall be able to separate us from the love of God, which is in Christ Jesus our Lord.

With the waters now lapping about her waist, she began to sing from the Psalter:

My sins and faults of youth
do thou, O Lord, forget;
After thy mercy think of me,
and for thy goodness great.

The air was rent with the cries and prayers of the towns-people, helpless to stop this gross miscarriage of justice. When the tide surged over Margaret's head, she retched. One of the soldiers stepped down into the rising waters and held her head above the surface.

"Just say 'God save the king,' " her mother pleaded.

Major Winram picked up where Mrs. Wilson left off. "Will you pray for the king?" he asked.

"I wish the salvation of all man and the damnation of none," Margaret replied.

"Say it, Margaret. Say 'God save the king!' " her mother begged again.

"God save him if he will. It is what I have prayed for in the past and what I do pray for now."

"We don't want your prayers," Grierson of Lagg barked. "We want to hear you swear the oath!"

"No! I cannot!" She turned to face the soldier holding up her head and spoke gently. "I am one of Christ's children. Let me go."

EPILOGUE

After the tide receded, the bodies of the two women were left tied to their stakes. Under cover of night, a few brave men carried them to the Wigtown kirkyard and buried them in a hastily dug grave. When the killing times ended, two stones were erected over the grave. One of them reads:

HERE LYES MARGRET LACHLANE WHO WAS
BY UNJUST LAW SENTENCED TO DIE BY
LAGG STRACHANE WINRAME AND GRHAME
AND TYED TO A STAKE WITHIN THE FLOOD
FOR HER ADHERENCE TO SCOTLANDS
REFORMATION COVENANTS NATIONAL AND
SOLEMN LEAGUE
AGED 63 1685

The stone commemorating Margaret Wilson's death reads:

LET EARTH AND STONE STILL WITNES BEARE
HEIR LYES A VIRGIN MARTYR HERE
MURTHERD FOR OUNING CHRIST SUPREME
HEAD OF HIS CHURCH AND NO MORE CRIME
BUT NOT ABJURING PRESRYTRY
AND HER NOT OUNING PRELACY
THEY HER CONDEM'D, BY UNJUST LAW,
OF HEAVEN NOR HELL THEY STOOD NO AW
WITHIN THE SEA TYD TO A STAKE

SHE SUFFERED FOR CHRIST JESUS SAKE.
THE ACTORS OF THIS CRUEL CRIME
WAS LAGG STRACHAN, WINRAM AND GRHAME
NEITHER YOUNG YEARES NOR YET OLD AGE
COULD STOP THE FURY OF THERE RAGE.

One of the most moving tributes to these brave Covenanters is the following poem.

The Martyrs of Wigtown

Long had they loved as Christians love
Those two so soon to die,
And each the other greeted first,
With weeping silently.
The matron wept that that young life
So timelessly must cease;
The maiden that that honoured head
Must not go down in peace.

But soon, O soon, it passed away
The coward thought and base,
And each looked humbly, thankfully,
Into the other's face.
"Mother, He rules the awful sea:
With all its waters wild."
"The many waters are His Voice
Of love to thee, my child."

Harriet Stuart Menteath

Author's Note

How Much of This Story Is True?

About twenty-five years ago, I read the words from Margaret Wilson's memorial stones in a book I was proofreading. That tribute to Margaret's faith impacted me so much that I've wanted to tell her story ever since. At times my research turned up conflicting accounts and variable spellings of names and places. I have presented Margaret's life according to those sources that seemed most reliable. Where there was a dearth of historical information, I created situations in keeping with life in southwestern Scotland in the seventeenth century.

The major incidents in this story are true, and all the characters were real people except for the Walkers and Margaret's Uncle Samuel and his sons. I have fictionalized a few portions of my story to enhance the plot while reflecting life in the seventeenth century. When my research did not turn up the kind of information I sought, I drew on my understanding of the times to create my tale. Sometimes I played with the timing of events to improve the flow of the story. It is true that James Renwick held a large conventicle at Old Risk castle. However, it was not held in the winter of 1685, nor was it attacked by the dragoons.

The Scots Presbyterians eventually won their battle with the coming of a new king. Today their church thrives not only in Scotland but also as the Reformed Presbyterian Church in North America.

WHAT HAPPENED TO MARGARET'S FAMILY?

Gilbert Wilson, though once one of the most substantial countrymen in Galloway, died in extreme poverty in 1689.

Janet Wilson lived to a great age on the charity of her friends.

Agnes Wilson. No records have been found about her after Margaret's death.

Thomas Wilson fled to Holland and served in the army of Prince William of Orange until 1689. Upon returning home, he became an elder in the kirk of Penninghame parish. He eventually married and moved to a farm in the Tig Valley.

A descendant of the Wilson family emigrated to America in the early nineteen century. From his lineage came **James Ruggles Wilson, D.D.**, professor of theology of the General Assembly of the Presbyterian Church of America. **Thomas Woodrow Wilson**, twenty-eighth president of the United States, was his son.

GLOSSARY

bairns: infants

bannock: a round, flat cake baked on a girdle

blether: talk foolishly or idly

bonnet: a soft, flat, brimless cap worn by men and boys

boot: an instrument of torture in which a prisoner's leg was crushed in a wooden frame

bracken: fern

braes: hills

brambles: blackberries

burgh: a town with special privileges, given it by a charter

burn: a brook or stream

byre: cattle shed

cairn: a heap of stones that served as a boundary marker or landmark

compear: to attend the local kirk (church) under compulsion

covenant: a solemn agreement made with God or Jesus

Covenanter: a person who made a covenant with God

conventicle: a secret meeting held for worship, prayer, and Bible study

divine right: the belief that God gives the king the authority to rule over the church

dragoon: a mounted soldier armed with a musket

fancy: to like, especially in a boy-girl relationship

girdle: a flat iron plate with a hooped handle that was hung over the fire for baking bannocks or oatcakes; now called a griddle

halberd: a combination spear and battle ax

Haud yer wheesht!: Be quiet!

kail: a cabbage-like vegetable with curly leaves; similar to kale

ken: know

kirk: church

kist: a chest for storing such things as oats that had been ground into meal

laird: landowner

moor: rough, uncultivated land, usually covered with heather and often marshy

moss-hag: a cut on the hillside, overhung with moss, heather, and other growths, from which peat has been removed

mutch: a close-fitting cap worn by married women

own: affirm

peat: partly decayed plant matter found in bogs. It was dried and used for fuel.

Psalter: a version of the psalms set to music and used as a hymnbook

quarter: to show mercy to an enemy; to house troops in the Covenanters' homes

skin (for buttermilk): the skinned hide of a calf or deer

snood: a hair ribbon tied at the back under the hair, worn by young unmarried women

steadings: the buildings and land that make up a farm

tolbooth: local jailhouse and place for doing business with the government (a courthouse)

TIMELINE

1638   Signing of the Scottish National Covenant

1643   Signing of the Solemn League and Covenant

1660   Charles II is restored as king, but he throws off his former allegiance to the Scottish Presbyterians.

1662   Ministers are turned out of their kirks for not accepting reappointment.

1667   Margaret Wilson is born in Glenvernoch.

1670   Conventicles are made treasonable, and preaching at them becomes a capital offense.

1679   Covenanters defeat the English forces at Drumclog on June 1.

        The Covenanters are defeated at Bothwell Bridge on June 22.

1684   Covenanters are forced to take the Test and swear the Abjuration Oath or face execution for refusal.

1685   The killing times—the period of hottest persecution

        Margaret is martyred on May 11.

        Accession of James II

1688   James Renwick becomes the last Covenanter to be publicly executed.

        The Glorious Revolution: The Presbyterian Church of Scotland is restored.

To Find Out More

You can find a complete annotated bibliography of the research materials used in writing *Against the Tide* on the author's website:

www.HopeIrvinMarston.com

Listed below are materials of special interest to young readers.

Bond, Douglas. Crown and Covenant Series, which includes *Duncan's War*, *King's Arrow*, and *Rebel's Keep*. Phillipsburg, N.J.: P&R Publishing, 2002, 2003, 2004.

Enock, Esther E. *Twelve Youthful Martyrs*. Salem, Ohio: Schmul Publishing, 1999.

Faris, Jerri. *Covenanters of Scotland: A History for Children*. Pittsburgh: Crown & Covenant Publications, 1995.

Howat, Irene. *Ten Girls Who Didn't Give In*. Ross-Shire, Scotland: Christian Focus Publications, 2005.

Love, Dane. *Scottish Covenanter Stories: Tales from the Killing Times*. Glasgow: Neil Wilson Publishing, 2000.

Mackenzie, Carine. *The Two Margarets*. Ross-Shire, Scotland: Christian Focus Publications, 1991.

Mackenzie, Catherine. *Danger on the Hill*. Ross-Shire, Scotland: Christian Focus Publications, 2003.

Maclean, George F. *Helen of the Glen: A Story of Christian Heroism.* Houston: Christian Focus Publications, 1988.

Orr, Brian J. *As God Is My witness: The Presbyterian Kirk, the Covenanters, and the Ulster Scots.* Bowie, MD: Heritage Books, 2002.

"Celtic Cry: The Heart of a Martyr." Produced by Brian Felten and J. Daniel Smith. Discovery House Music, 2002. CD and videocassette.

"The Covenanters. The Fifty Years Struggle 1638–1688.": *www.sorbie.net/covenanters.htm.*

"The Scottish Covenanters." Produced by Ichthus Ministries with Christian Faith Ministries, Scotland. VHS. Distributed by Gateway Films-Vision Video, Box 540, Worcester, PA, 1998.

Hope Irvin Marston, a retired English teacher and librarian, is the author of more than two dozen children's books. *Against the Tide: The Valor of Margaret Wilson* is her first historical novel. Her other titles include a daily devotional book, photographic essays on large machines (big rigs, fire trucks, snowplows, ambulances, farm machinery, cranes, and derricks), a biography, and wildlife picture books. She holds an M.A. in library science from Milligan College (TN). She lives with her husband and their Bernese Mountain Dog near Fort Drum in upstate New York. Please visit the author online at: *www.HopeIrvinMarston.com.*